THE BOBTAILS MEET THE PREACHER'S KID

BOBTAILS ADVENTURES
BOOK 1

ARTHUR YEOMANS

WISE PATH
BOOKS

ISBNs:

978-1-959666-02-8 (paperback)

978-1-959666-03-5 (ebook)

Published by:

Wise Path Books

a division of To A Finish LLC

12407 N MoPac Expy #250

Austin, TX 78758

www.wisepathbooks.com

CONTENTS

To my Grandson Daniel,
who said he liked it,
and to the authors of such books as:

- *Swallows and Amazons*
- *Anne of Green Gables*
- *Little Britches*
- *Captains Courageous*
- *Understood Betsy*
- *The Sugar Creek Gang (original editions)*

From whom I cheerfully stole many of the concepts and even names.

With special thanks to my wife, who suffered through dozens of versions. And to my illustrators: Matt, Kat, Lilly, Gwen, Esther, and Grace. And to my Alpha Reader: David.

"If you want a thing done well, do it yourself."
— ***Napoleon Bonaparte***

G race Livingston, Mrs Grace Livingston, although her husband had been dead these five years, stood up and reached for her bag from the overhead compartment, then sat down again in her seat. Her stop was coming up, and she wanted to be ready.

She looked around the cabin again. It was certainly very dingy. As was normal for trains, it was all over coal dust. And the seat covers were hopelessly faded. She supposed none of that mattered as long as it accomplished its task of taking people from place to place.

The compartment was relatively empty. The young lady sitting across from her had a silly grin on her face, so Grace expected she was on her way to meet some young gentleman; or whatever passed for a young gentleman in this town.

She felt sorry for the young mother riding with two children, sitting in the set of seats to her left. Her children had been whining the whole time despite their mother's admonition. She had obviously been poorly trained herself, and didn't realise she was encouraging their bad behaviour by talking to them instead of administering discipline.

These had been her companions for the past ten miles and, indeed, the only people she had seen except for the rather harassed conductor who passed through their wagon from time to time. She did not imagine he was very efficient at his job from how he seemed to have to go to and fro frequently and from the frustrated look on his face.

She had not enjoyed this train ride, but then, she hadn't expected to. What she enjoyed was getting her work done on her farm, not taking train rides. And certainly, the occasion of this train ride, the death of her sister and her sister's husband, was nothing she enjoyed.

She had not been able to see her sister often, they had lived too far from each other for that, but they had written to each other faithfully every week... an activity that Grace allowed herself to do on Sundays... and since Grace's husband had died her sister had been her closest relative. Indeed her closest contact of any kind, she supposed.

Their death had been a tragic shock, one which she didn't suppose she would ever get over. Some gas explosion. Thank the Lord the children had been visiting friends.

The children. Her sister had had four children. In Grace's opinion, they were the best raised of all of her niblings.[1] Robert's children were quieter, they wouldn't dare to be anything else, but they were lacking in life. John's children, like John himself, were totally lacking in self-discipline. Roger had lovely children, but there were so many of them they were almost raising themselves.

Her sister's children didn't like her; Grace knew that. She hadn't ever seen it as her business to foster a relationship with them. She hadn't gone out of her way to make herself attractive to them. She had her life, and they had theirs; they had been well-behaved when she had visited and thus had never annoyed her. But Susan's children were now orphans, and what was to become of them?

Well, she had three brothers, and they were all married with children of their own, so one of them would no doubt do for the children.

She stared out the window, attempting to take her mind off her sister. The train was slowing down, and she could see it was moving through a quiet part of town with tall buildings, mostly made of red brick. No real flora, just an occasional park and, poor things, some trees set into holes in the pavement, struggling to survive.

While she thought, she descended from the train and, ignoring the bustling crowds on the platform, looked around and there, on the wall, was a map. A few seconds of perusal and she verified the directions she had been sent by telegram. The meeting with the judge was going to be in a lawyer's office, as that law firm was handling the inheritance, and their office was located just down the street from the train station. Very convenient and no doubt good for their business.

She stepped smartly down the ugly city street—she found all city streets ugly—and down the two blocks to the office.

She paused outside the door to put her thoughts aside and then stepped briskly up the two flights to the office. Arriving at an anteroom, she went up to the girl sitting behind the counter. "I am Grace Livingston, nee Barker, and I was requested to come here for a meeting with the judge concerning my sister's estate. My sister and her husband. They died three weeks ago, on March 21, 1889."

"Ah, yes, Mrs Livingston," The girl said, looking down at a large book in front of her. "The meeting will be in our conference room; allow me to show you the way."

Grace stepped briskly after the girl down a corridor. A young, healthy-looking girl, although she would look healthier without her face paint. She pitied her, having to work in an office. She hoped she would get married soon and get to manage her own house. She looked decent enough for some man to snap up. Hopefully, she wouldn't carry on with her boss the way Grace had heard happened in the cities. Or perhaps she was already married, and her husband had her working here!

"Right here," the girl said, opening a door and ushering her in. "We have coffee and fritters on that sideboard, and if you need anything else, feel free to ask me."

Grace thanked her and then, with a moment's hesitation, went over to the sideboard. This was a business meeting, and she hated to look as if she was here to socialise, but they had set it out, and she had had a long train ride and was hungry.

She had just gotten her coffee and a strawberry fritter, at least she hoped it was strawberry, and sat down, when John and Robert walked in, arguing.

"I don't think I am," John was saying. "You know they didn't leave much money and... Oh, Grace, how are you doing?"

"As well as can be expected under the circumstances, John. And how are Lilly and the children?"

"Well, Lilly is especially devastated. She has such a tender heart."

A tender heart and a tender head, in Grace's opinion, but no particular good could be done by saying so here. "And you, Robert?"

Robert, her oldest brother and by far the most well-off, nodded. "We are all most upset by this tragedy, naturally. I have my lawyers looking into the matter, I quite assure you. Such criminal negligence."

No doubt he and his lawyers would find some way to get money out of it. Which, to be fair, he would direct toward his niblings, as was only right and proper, paying them back in some small measure for the tragic death of their parents.

Just then, Roger walked in, looking preoccupied as usual. He didn't say anything but came up and hugged Grace, which she returned. Not much of a talker but very physical, Roger. No doubt why he had so many children.

But before she had time to say anything to him, an older man walked in, looking every inch the judge in his black robes. Everyone immediately sat down, and the room grew still.

"I suppose we are all here? You are Mrs Livingston, the surviving sister?"

Grace nodded, seeing no reason to speak. This conference wasn't about her.

"And you, Sir, are Robert? The oldest brother?"

"Yes, quite," Robert said.

"And you are John, the twin of the deceased?"

John nodded, his eyes dimming.

"And Roger, the youngest brother."

Roger whispered a quiet "Yes."

"To start with, I wish to express my deepest condolences," the judge began. "I didn't know your sister and her husband, but everything I have heard tells me that their death is a great loss."

"And certainly the greatest loss will be felt by their children, now orphans. Our first goal today is to determine their placement. I understand, Sir, that they are staying with you?"

Robert looked pleased to be noticed and nodded. "Yes, quite. We live closest, as you know, and the minute we were informed of the tragedy, I naturally went over and collected the grieving children and brought them to my house."

"And do you think that it would be good for them to stay with you long-term?"

Robert flushed. "Well, well, no, I don't. I, well, I am the Vice President of a bank, and my job often involves long hours. I do my duty to my own children, but it seems to me that, well, recently orphaned children will take an extraordinary amount of, as it were, care or attention for the foreseeable future and in my case, that might be difficult."

"I see," the judge said with a slight frown. He turned to John. "And you, Sir?"

John frowned, looking at Robert. "Robert feels that we would be the best. And we love the children; we love them dearly. But four new children... to put it bluntly, we lack the means. The financial means, that is. We are already packed very tightly into our house, and I simply don't have the means for an addition. I don't think it would be fair to them to put them in such a condition."

The judge nodded and turned to Roger, who blushed.

"We love children," he said very quietly. "We would, of course, love to have them..."

"Seriously, Roger, how can you say such a thing?" Robert said. "I can't deny you have the room, but you already have twelve of your own... I can't even keep track of their names. Your poor wife."

"Well, we would love to have them," Roger said, " but I don't deny that, as you say, Robert, they will probably take a lot of extra care in the beginning. And our Cynthia..."

"His daughter had polio," Robert said, turning to the judge. "She is the nicest girl in all the world, but, as he says, she takes a lot of extra care. No, seriously, John, I think that..."

"But how could we..."

Grace spent an annoying few seconds listening to her brothers arguing. Roger wasn't saying anything but was almost crying; Robert looked trapped, and John, poor John, literally poor John...

"I'll take them!" she said loudly.

The entire room turned to her, shocked.

"But Grace, you aren't married!" John said. "I mean... you were... but..."

"And if I was a widow and they were my children would you take them from me?" she asked tartly.

Robert looked appalled, John looked embarrassed, and Roger looked at her with wondering eyes and a bit of a grin.

"I would have to approve any such placement," the judge said, rather austerely, "and I don't often approve of placements with, umm, households without two parents in them."

"That is not to say..." he said, looking at her brothers, and stroking his long beard meditatively, "That is not to say it is out of the question. I could, indeed I would, make any such placement under probation. Can you tell me, Mrs Livingston, of your circumstances?"

"Certainly!" she said. "I did not come here to insist on having the children; I don't at all think it is best for a woman living alone to raise children. But, given our current circumstances, I think it is best."

"I am a widow of five years. We never had any children of our own, but not from lack of desire!"

"I own, with no debt to any bank, a perfectly adequate house of three bedrooms on a small farm, which I run as a cheese-making business. My husband left me a bit of an income from his investments, but I rarely have to use that money and never dip into the capital. I am largely self-sufficient in other ways, with a house garden, chickens, a few geese, and I usually butcher two hogs...that is, I have some men and boys come in and help me butcher two, or sometimes three, hogs every winter. I certainly don't lack food."

"So, you live in the country."

"Yes. That is, there is a small town within easy walking distance, and a school. Which has a very good reputation. And a church."

"I see," said the judge. "And keeping that farm, you would have time for the children?"

"Certainly! Indeed there is nothing better for children than to work around a farm."

"Quite," the judge said.

While the judge was musing on his next question, Robert leaned over the table. "Now, Grace. You know that young Robert..." he looked at the Judge, "... my brother-in-law named two of his children after Roger and I. I think he was hoping for a third son to name John. Grace, you know that young Robert is eleven years old. He isn't a strong-willed child, nothing wild, but he will still need discipline from time to time... do you think..."

"Seriously, Robert, do you know me at all? I will have no problem at all taking him to the woodshed. And if he should turn too wild to follow me there, which I don't expect, I have plenty of men as neighbours whom I won't hesitate to call."

"She has never hesitated to lick any of mine," Roger put in. He grinned. "They still talk about that time when she caught my Gregory with a cigar. He couldn't sit down for a week."

Robert nodded but continued, "Well, Grace, I hate to bring it up, but... well, you know that the children... you aren't exactly their favourite person."

"I know that, Robert. But what they need right now is not some favourite person, but someone who has the time..." she stared at Robert, "The money," John blushed, "And, well, the energy," she said, as Roger grinned at her, "To take care of them. They need to get back on their feet after this terrible tragedy, and I think I am the one best to accomplish that."

She sat back, folded her arms and stared at them, shocked that she had said any such thing and, all the more, that she firmly believed it. She hadn't dreamed, coming here, that she would insist on having the children but now... The children needed—her sister's children needed a stable atmosphere, a strong hand, good boundaries, lots of work to take their minds off of...

Before she could turn maudlin, she raised her eyes and stared at the judge, whom she found was studying her.

He turned his eyes from her and gave a look around the room, then slowly nodded. "I am inclined to agree. Now let us work out how that is to be accomplished. They shouldn't leave right away; there are still some matters to be worked out..."

Right is right even if nobody does it.
Wrong is wrong even if everybody is wrong about it.
— ***Gilbert K. Chesterton***

Chapter One

THE TRAIN

Esther sat on this very loud and dirty train, watching Roger, her younger brother. Roger was bouncing up and down in his seat and looking out the train window, which he did whenever he wasn't running up and down the aisles or going off to see if the conductor would let him visit the engine. Or eating. Well, no, he would look out the window when eating; he just would mostly stop bouncing.

Her little sister Ruth was in her seat, asleep, her two middle fingers stuck firmly in her mouth. Her frock was all askew, but Esther didn't think it worth waking her to fix it. And it was rather messy from the breakfast that Aunt Rosemary had sent with them.

She sat with her oldest brother, Robert, who was cleaner but, like all of them, his clothes had acquired a coating of coal dust, which came rushing in any time the windows or doors were open. The shabby red coverings to the seats were coated with black dust, which fell down whenever anyone took anything from the overhead compartments.

She fingered her dress. Other than her siblings, the only thing left from her life before the explosion. Her brothers had worn old clothes to play with the neighbours, and her sister's frock from that day was in her bag, but Esther had chosen to wear this frock today rather than any of the ones Uncle Robert had bought them.

Roger bounced out of his seat and started toward the aisle. "Where are you going?" Esther asked him.

"Hafta go," Roger said, holding himself.

Esther darted a glance at Robert, who didn't seem inclined to get up. "I'll take you," Esther said, starting to get up.

"Don't need help," Roger said. "Know where it is, just two cars up, know how to do my pants myself!"

"Oh, very well," Esther said, and Roger, grinning, raced off up the aisle.

"I don't know why we couldn't have stayed with Uncle John," Esther said, turning to Robert. "He likes us. His kids like us. And Aunt Lilly is nice."

"He's too poor," Robert said. "And Uncle Robert is too busy."

"We could have gone with Uncle Roger," Esther said, a bit doubtfully.

Robert was silent for a minute. "We could've. It isn't like he doesn't know about adopting children; he adopted his first five when he married Aunt Lydia. But they have twelve kids... I think everyone might have thought we would get lost in the crowd. So we ended up with the witch."

"Robert, you mustn't say that," Esther protested. Although she was a year and a half younger than Robert and deferred to him on most things, she still had a very firm idea of proper propriety and was inclined to correct his language and dress, which he tolerated.

"Well, we've always called her that," he said. "You have called her that. With her sharp nose, sharp eyes, sharp voice, and always wearing black and white with those big black boots and that black hat."

"At home..." Esther said, tearing up. Robert pretended not to see her dab her eyes and waited for her to finish. "... but now we are going to live with her, we must be properly respectful."

"I'm sure she'll see to that," Robert said. "She's all the one for proper behaviour."

Esther cocked her head quizzically, and he hurriedly corrected, "Well, I'm not saying she dresses fancy, and she isn't diplomatic in her speaking; she is the loudest walker I have known... but she doesn't let you step the least bit out of line about anything she cares about, and you daren't be late."

"Oh, well, yes." She giggled, "She is the funniest dresser. But to be fair, I think she only really has the one town outfit."

She looked at Ruth, "Oh, Robert... how are we going to manage?"

"We will have to be there for each other. Or, you and I will. Roger will be fine, I think. He wet the bed last night," he said, leaning over close to her and whispering, "but I just took the sheets to Aunty and didn't say anything, and you couldn't tell from the way he carried on."

Esther grinned, "Poor Aunty, she loves us, but she will be very glad we are gone. And the cousins... we rather upset their boring oh-so-regular little lives. Can you imagine? One boy, one girl, each with his own room, his own desk, and his own bookshelf..."

Robert grinned, "And we come in and uncle rents some cots, buys us a whole mess of clothes, and we're all over their room and all into their stuff, and Roger was forever borrowing books and putting them back all willy nilly."

Esther looked wistful, "They did have some very nice books."

"That they did. But I'm sure Uncle will buy us some if we

write him. He looked positively guilty when he put us on the train."

Roger came racing back in, still fumbling with the buttons on his pants, and Esther sat back and looked around the compartment again. The man sitting near the door was wearing an interesting suit, a brown check with a bright orange tie, which Esther didn't think quite went.

Just then the train boy came back in. The boy whom Robert had told her worked on the train selling things and who was called a 'butcher'. He wore a black and white suit and had two straps over his shoulder, which helped him hold up a big tray in front of him full of stuff which he was selling. There was a big grin on his face even though they hadn't bought anything from him.

Roger ran up to the boy, looking at his tray. "What kind of chocolate you got?"

"Lots," the boy said. "Cadbury's the most expensive."

"What's the cheapest?"

"Plain wrap."

"Robert, can we...?"

"No, I've told you, buying on the train is too expensive. We will get some when we get off the train at a regular store."

"Good try, mate," the boy grinned, tousled Roger's hair and moved on through the wagon.

"Roger, sit down and stop bothering people," Esther said as Roger remained standing in the aisle.

"I wasn't bothering him."

"Perhaps not, but you're bothering everyone else. Now sit down!"

Roger went and plunked himself down by the window. "Oh, good, another train is coming!"

"Roger, come here this minute," Robert said. Roger was at the other end of the train staring out the window, and he ignored Robert and kept staring out the back window until a gentleman sitting next to where he was standing clouted him on the head. Then Roger put one heel down and, pushing with his other foot, spun in place and came grinning over to Robert.

"Get your bag down," Robert commanded. "And Esther's. I've already got mine and Ruth's, and Esther's got Ruth, so you need to carry your things and hers."

Roger sprang upon the seat and reached the bags down. "What are we doing?" he asked.

"Changing trains, dinkus, as you would know if you had been paying the least bit of attention when the conductor put us on..."

Roger grinned, and just then, as if he had heard himself mentioned, the conductor came hurrying in, looking anxiously around. Seeing them standing by the door, all of them together with their bags, he looked relieved. The poor man seemed to find it rather stressful to have children in his care. He had come through every few minutes and always seemed almost surprised that none of them had fallen off the train yet.

"Time to change trains, children," he said. " We'll be at the station in ten minutes, and I'll put you in the charge of the baggage handler, which he'll talk to you after he moves the bags. You all stay put where I put you until he comes."

Robert stood at the door and watched the buildings go by. Mostly fields, but there were some interesting silos, all painted differently. This area of the track must not be well maintained; the train was rattling something awful.

He grabbed the railing and leaned forward to look at a simply enormous barn. It must be at least four stories tall. What did they do with it besides keep animals in it? One thing he was looking forward to at Aunt Grace's house was getting to see her barns and all. How many animals did she keep at her dairy?

Then he looked forward and saw the station coming up. It was one of the biggest stations they had yet seen, with two stories and a large open wooden platform. There were lots of benches on the platform and gas lights. Oh, and an enormous clock rising up above the whole thing, which read 10:59.

The train slowed, and they passed a dozen or so wagons, all waiting for cargo. And then the train eased up to the platform, and the conductor came hurrying back into their wagon. "Follow me!" he said.

They followed him off the train, ahead of the crowd of people that were getting off, and he waved them over to a bench. "You all stay there until he comes for you."

"I hope he will give us something to eat," Roger said as he slung his bag under the bench and, going to the back of it, started pulling himself over and putting his hands down to do a handstand. "I'm hungry."

"You are always hungry," Esther said, sitting down and pulling Ruth onto her lap.

"I'm a growing boy," Roger declared, and then crashed to the ground.

"Roger!" Esther started to say, but Robert held up his hand.

"Let him play," he said. "He needs the fresh air and some exercise. It's nice that it is warm enough for him to play."

"He seems to get quite enough exercise," Esther said, but she didn't say anything as Roger went around the bench to try again. "How long are we going to be here?"

"We have an hour till our next train comes in," Robert said. "When the baggage man comes I'm going to go off and try to find something to buy to eat. Uncle Robert gave me two whole dollars for the trip, which our dinners shouldn't even come close to touching."

"He probably meant you to save some of it," she said. "You know... 'a penny saved'."

"I should be able to save more than a penny," Robert said. "I see a store down there where I can get them to make us up sandwiches, and I can get some apples and some milk... I doubt it will all cost a quarter."

"Get some cheese for later in the trip," Esther said.

"And chocolate!" Roger said, picking himself up from his latest fall. "I'll come with you to make sure you get a good kind."

Robert looked at Esther, who nodded. "Ruth and I will watch the luggage. We might even walk up and down a bit; I think it will be good for her."

"Good for you, too," Roger said, mounting for his third try. "All sitting and no walking makes a dull Esther... Hey!"

"Well!" Esther said, "You did do it. Look, Ruth, look at Roger doing a handstand..."

Ruth looked and giggled as Roger came crashing back down to the ground, then went back to putting her fingers in her mouth and clinging to Esther.

"Good job, Roger," Robert said. "Oh, good, maybe this is the baggage handler."

The others all looked and saw a large man with an enormous beard coming up to them, a grin on his face. He was wearing a bright red uniform which would have been brighter red if it hadn't been so dirty.

"So, you're my 11:45 children, are you? Four of you, are there? Well, be back in this seat by 11:30 cause I don't want to hunt you down. No playing with the baggage, and don't bother the station master; he's a busy man."

He said this last, looking at Roger, almost as if he knew that that was the kind of thing Roger had been doing the whole trip. "A busy man with a quick cane for the backside of bothersome children," the baggage handler added. "Now, mind you're back by 11:30."

The baggage handler left, and Robert turned to go to the store. Roger raced past him, and Robert turned to ask Esther if she thought they should get some milk. But she had her handkerchief out, and, not wanting to see her cry, Robert decided to just get the milk and hurried off.

Roger, who would have been caught dead before being caught crying, raced ahead of Robert up the road. He dashed past the store, stopped, spun, and raced back to the front door before Robert got there and waited for him to come up. Then he went in after him. Roger would much rather that Robert go first and meet people or whatever.

"Good morning, ma'am," Roger heard his brother say as he looked at some interesting tops they had, "Can I get some sandwiches made up?"

Roger didn't hear the answer, being too busy on his hands and knees looking at a selection of books, but he heard his brother when he said, "Roger? Do you want meat and cheese sandwiches? Or butter and jam?"

Roger liked butter and jam better, but meat and cheese lasted longer, so he said, "Two meat and one jam."

"Three? Oh, very well, " his brother said, and Roger went back to looking at the books.

"Robert? Could I buy a book?"

"You mean, could I buy you a book," Robert said, coming up. "It must be a book to share, and it can't cost too much, but it seems a wise purchase."

Roger dove back down to the ground, not bothering to

argue. "Here's a Henty!" he said triumphantly. "You could read that to all of us!"

"Well," Robert said, turning it over, "I suppose I could. Ma'am, how much is this book?"

Roger ignored the negotiations but suddenly remembered. "What chocolate did you get?"

"That was your job," Robert said, pointing to a rack.

Roger raced over and looked at the chocolate very carefully. He wanted to buy small packages so he could eat a whole package and still have some other packages left. And Esther wouldn't think a whole package too big for him to eat all at once. And he wanted a variety, but all ones he liked, so if someone else didn't like one, he didn't mind getting stuck with it.

Robert seemed like he was getting impatient, so Roger chose a dozen packages of three different kinds and quickly put them on the counter.

"That's so many..." Robert said, staring doubtfully at the candy.

"They're small," Roger insisted, and the clerk, quickly wrapping them up, said,

"Cheaper by the dozen. Here are your sandwiches, your book, your cheese, your chocolates; pick up the milk from the cooler on your way out and don't forget to send the boy back with the bottles, one dollar ten cents."

Roger watched anxiously as Robert hesitated and then handed her the money. "Well, we did get enough for two meals, and we did get milk. And a book, which was expensive."

"You carry the book back," Robert said, handing it to him, "And show it to the girls. It was your idea."

Roger took the book and, walking carefully out of the store, started racing back as soon he hit the boardwalk. "Girls, look what Robert bought us!" he said, racing up.

"What?" Esther said. "He needs to be careful spending... oh, a book? A Henty? We haven't read this one... no... I don't think we have. Oh, Roger, that is wonderful."

"I found it," Roger said, grinning.

"And it was his idea to buy it, too," Robert said. "Now, let us pray so we can eat."

Robert felt a hand shaking him. "Wake up, young Sir," he heard and opened his bleary eyes to see the conductor shaking him. "We're almost there, and I'm sure you will need some time to get your siblings ready. It's gotten a bit colder; it always does for spring in these parts. Hot days and cool evenings."

Robert forgot for a few seconds where he was and what

they were doing and just stared around, confused. But then he saw Ruth asleep in Esther's lap, and everything came crashing back on him. Their parent's death. The awkward time with Uncle Robert. The train ride. And now...

"Thank you, Sir," he said, sitting up.

The conductor nodded and went off, and Robert reached over and shook Esther, who woke, looked around, and said, "Oh, did I fall asleep? I'm sorry."

"We all fell asleep," he said, going over to Roger who was sprawled out over three seats and shook him.

"There yet?" Roger asked, springing awake and looking out the window.

"Almost," Robert said. "The conductor said we'll need our coats. Roger..." he started to say, but his brother had already sprung up on the seat and, almost stepping on Esther and Ruth, quick handed all of their bags down to the others.

Esther took Ruth's coat and tried to put it on her very gently, but Ruth woke up and looked around. And didn't even cry! Robert never could tell what she was feeling when she looked like that. Was she afraid? Curious? She hadn't spoken much before mother and father died, and she said almost nothing now.

Esther put her down and stood up to put on her own coat, hat, and mittens. Robert thought that a bit too far, so he put his hat and mittens in his coat pocket.

Roger had found some chocolate in his coat pocket and was busy eating it and looking out the window. "There's the station!" he said, pointing, and Robert, Esther, and Ruth all looked out the window.

The station was much smaller than the one they had changed trains in, indeed one of the smallest they had yet seen. It was made all out of bricks, except for one wall toward the front which was made of planks. It just had a small clock on a pole as they came up and had a small covered wooden platform in front of it, where the train tracks came up close. Several wagons stood in the yard right before the station, with men sitting on the wagons.

Standing in the middle of the small platform, right under the sign, and all alone except for a baggage handler in the same red uniform as the one that had put them on this train, was a tall woman wearing a long black skirt, boots, and a red plaid flannel shirt. She was staring at the train with her lips set in a kind of determined frown and her arms crossed across her chest.

"There she is," Esther said. "Aunt Grace."

"She's not wearing a coat!" Roger accused. "Why did we have to put them on?"

"She must be used to it," Robert said. "And hasn't been in a warm train car for the last few hours."

"It is hot in here," Roger agreed. "I'll be glad to get out into the air again."

He peered out the window again as the train drew closer and closer to the station, slowing all the time. "She doesn't look much like a witch with that shirt on," he declared. Who ever heard of a witch wearing red flannel plaid?

Ruth giggled, and Esther grinned.

"No broomstick either," Roger said, grinning.

"Oh!" Robert said, suddenly realising, "We completely forgot to read our new Henty! I'm so sorry. I hope we will get some time to do so at Aunty's."

No one answered him. They all stood looking out of the window as the train slowed down and then, finally, stopped with a great huff of noise and steam and all. Robert saw that Esther and Roger were both hanging back, so, trying his best to be a man, he went forward to be first off the train; the first to greet Aunt Grace, who would be taking care of them.

"There you are!" Aunt Grace said, lowering her hands, her

frown relaxing a bit. She strode forward from where she had been waiting. "And you all look like you stood the trip well."

She reached forward and, without even a by your leave, plucked Ruth out of Esther's arms. Esther looked as if she would cry, but Ruth merely clung to her aunt and looked sleepily around.

"My buggy is over here," Aunt Grace said, turning toward the yard. "Robert, do you know how to drive a buggy?"

Robert, startled, let out a small squeak and then managed, "No, ma'am."

"Well, that's a shame. You will have to learn. You will all have to learn. It's an important skill. Well, follow me."

Robert, dazed, realised that if he had answered 'yes,' he would have been driving the buggy home. He saw his aunt getting well ahead of him and caught up just as Roger came over to her and said, "I need to water the bushes!"

"Well, there are plenty of bushes," his aunt said. "And there is an outhouse if you need to... put your bags in the buggy first, Roger!" She called, as Roger had just dropped the bags he was carrying and started racing off to the bushes. Roger raced back, grabbed both bags, raced over to the only buggy in the yard, threw them in the back, and then raced off to the bushes fumbling with his pants along the way.

Robert watched Aunt Grace to see if she blushed the way Aunt Rosemary might have, but she ignored Roger and brusquely helped Esther into the back, handing her back Ruth, who quickly crawled into Esther's lap. Then Aunt Grace took Robert's bags, put them next to Esther, and waved Robert to the front before he had a chance to crawl in the back. As he climbed up, he wished he had been brave enough to ask to use the bushes. Now he would have to wait till they got to the house. "Time and tide wait for no man," his father would have said.

"It isn't hard," Aunt Grace said, handing him the reins.

"You pull the rein gently—these are well-trained horses—the way you want to go and..."

Just at that moment, Roger came leaping up into the front next to Robert and looked jealously at the reins. "Pay attention, Roger, and you will be next," Aunt Grace said, and Roger's eyes about bugged out of his face.

"Now, as I was saying, pull the rein the way you want to go. Now, Roger, say 'Gee up'."

Roger said 'Gee up' with considerable force, but Aunt Grace didn't comment, and the horses started. "Out of the yard and to the left, please, Robert," Aunt Grace said, and Robert had a moment's panic as he tried to figure out when to pull on the reins, but before they got too far, he pulled gently on the left rein and led them out of the yard.

" Very good," his aunt said. "Now we go on this way for two miles, then you'll see a large, burnt, oak tree on the right; turn there."

Robert's heart pounded but there was really nothing easier than sitting here doing nothing with these reins as the horses plodded forward down a road they had no doubt been down dozens of times before. The sun was just going down, but there was still plenty of light. And it was getting cooler as he drove.

"Have you all eaten?" Aunt Grace asked.

"Oh, yes, ma'am," Robert said. "Uncle Robert gave me two whole dollars for trip expenses, and I bought sandwiches, milk, and cheese which we ate for dinner and supper."

"Not the milk," Roger said. "Which we had to take the bottles back before we even left the station."

"And we had chocolate," Robert added.

"Well, that's good. It's rather late and I think it will be good if you go straight to bed. Travelling can be tiring. I know I was tired when I got home from meeting with the judge."

"We were surprised that you were taking us," Roger said, making Robert blush. His brother could be so... brash?

"To tell you the truth, Roger, I was surprised myself. Very surprised. But I think it will be for the best."

Roger spun and started looking at the landscape they were passing, and Robert concentrated on his driving, which involved some long, slow turns back and forth. His heart began pounding again when he recognised the large, burnt, oak and then as he made the turn: which he took a bit wide, but, really, this driving a buggy wasn't hard.

"Now, Roger, your turn," his Aunt said when Robert had straightened out from the turn, and Robert handed Roger the reins.

All the business of war, and indeed all the business of life, is to endeavour to find out what you don't know by what you do; that's what I called 'guess what was at the other side of the hill'.

—Duke of Wellington

Chapter Two

THE HOUSE

Roger watched the house coming up, which Aunt Grace had told him it was this one, excited and nervous at the same time. He was driving the buggy and he would be the one to pull on the reins to stop the horses! But now he was coming up on a strange house, with a strange bed in a strange bedroom, and his very strange aunt who was not his mother. Who everyone told him was dead but who he firmly expected to wake him up in the morning.

But then he looked out at the area around him, and he got really, really, excited. They were passing some fields with just grass growing in them and another with big fences and a few horses, including one little horse. And just past the fields with the horses was a line of trees. They had passed lots of trees like that, and every time there had also been a creek, or even a small river. Past the trees, a ways away, were some hills which looked really fun to climb.

And the noises were wonderful. Everything was all quiet except for their own horses and the buggy he was driving. He was driving! The horses made wonderful clop clop noises, so different from the rattle rattle of the train, and the buggy made crunching noises going over the ground and squeak squeak noises as it went up and down, which it did quite a lot as this road was not all smooth and flat like he was used to. And it was that perfect time of day when it was dark but not too dark to see.

He was so busy thinking that he almost but not quite allowed the horses to go past the front door. He pulled on the reins, and they stopped.

He threw the reins over the front of the buggy, leapt down and was halfway to the door when his aunt called to him, "Roger! You have bags to bring in!"

She had a very sharp voice, his aunt. Which was good. He didn't want her to have a voice like his mother. Because she wasn't his mother. She was his aunt, and his mother would be waking him up in the morning. Or if not this morning, then the next one.

He raced back, grabbed the bags and still managed to be first at the door, which he opened and went through, and almost forgot to hold open for the others.

"Take the bags upstairs, Roger," his aunt said, and Roger looked around, saw a very narrow set of stairs, and raced up them. It was a wonderful, fun set of stairs, all narrow and dark, and half the steps squeaked when he stepped on them, and his boots made bangs on each of them.

At the top of the stairs was a tiny hallway, not really a hallway at all, just a little open area with three doors. He opened the door to the right and closed it again quickly. That was obviously his aunt's room; it had girl clothes hanging in the wardrobe.

He opened the first door on the other side, but if it was his room, his aunt had a strange idea of housekeeping... everything was all covered with sheets. Probably the guest room, and he was sure his Aunt would never let him play in there.

The third door opened onto another bedroom. This must

be his and Robert's room; he saw the trunk that Uncle Robert had bought them just as he walked in, but where was he to sleep? There was a lantern on a shelf on the wall, a couch, a wardrobe, a dresser, a ladder to the attic in one corner... but only one bed... he spun around and around in the room wondering. Would they have to share the bed? It was big enough.

"Roger!" He heard and spun back toward the door and raced back out and into his Aunt's room, the room with the girl clothes, where the others were. "Leave Esther's bag here," Aunt Grace directed, pointing at the floor near the wardrobe.

Roger plunked the bag down and spun around to watch his aunt. His aunt they would be staying with, who was not his mother.

"The girls will be sleeping here with me," she said. "Esther, you will sleep in the bed with me. Ruth will sleep in that cot," she said, pointing to a small cot which was pretty perfectly Ruth's size in a corner. "Esther, I will go and explain things to the boys; you put Ruth down for tonight."

Roger followed his aunt out, and sure enough, she went to the room he had been sure was his and Robert's. "Robert, Roger, this is your room. Robert, as the oldest, you will have the bed. Roger, you will sleep on the couch."

Roger spun, astonished, to the couch and then spun back to stare at his aunt. Was she kidding? Did he really get to sleep on the couch? All of his life he had liked sleeping in strange places, or, at least, places other people thought strange.

But, no, she wasn't kidding. She fixed him with a firm stare and stalked out of their room and down the stairs, her boots clumping loudly the way his aunt's boots always did, which everyone else thought was funny but he liked.

"I'm sorry," Robert began. "I can..."

"Don't you dare!" Roger said, beginning to rip off his

clothes. "I love it. Where is my...?" He spun round until, in one corner, he saw the trunk that Uncle Robert had sent, which he had seen before but had forgotten in the excitement of getting to sleep on the couch, the trunk which contained all of the clothes that Uncle Robert had bought for them except for the two sets they had carried on the train.

He dashed over to the trunk and, after lifting the heavy lid, found a nightshirt and, after throwing that on, spotted a pile, a very neat pile, of sheets and blankets on the end of the couch, which he hadn't noticed before. He went over and pulled them on his new bed.

As he pulled them on, he heard Esther talking in the next room. When she talked with Ruth, she always tried to make her voice all soft and sweet and motherly. It was kind of funny, but Ruth really liked it. Ruth liked Roger, too, but mostly to laugh at. He liked making her laugh. It was a good thing that she had him during this time with their parents not there.

He pulled the sheets and blankets onto his bed, at first all cattywampus but then, fearing his aunt would come back and 'fix' them, he pulled them back off and laid them more neatly. Then he rolled his pants up, stuffed them in his shirt, and arranged it for a pillow. Then he took his coat, climbed into his bed, put the coat over his head...

"Have you said your prayers, Roger?" He heard Aunt Grace ask and, sliding out of his wonderful new bed he quickly kneeled down and said the prayer that his mother had taught him. He didn't want his aunt, who wasn't his mother, trying to pray with him.

He finished and quickly crawled back in. He covered his head with his coat and, as no one said anything or asked him to do anything else, dreamed of all the exploring he would do tomorrow... and fell asleep.

Esther sleepily felt a stir next to her, and then the bed shook, and she heard feet hitting the floor. "Esther," she heard her aunt say, "It is time for you and me to get up."

Esther got quickly out of bed, rather gasping when her feet hit the hardwood floor. It was cold!

She went over to Ruth, who was still sleeping, her mouth open and drooling. Her covers were half off, which Esther quickly fixed, gazing at her little sister and hoping she would do well. She, Esther, would have to make sure she did. She would have to watch out for her, which meant making sure that Aunt was not mad at her.

So she left off looking at Ruth, went over to her trunk, got out long undergarments and a working dress, and, shivering, went and sat on the bed, pulling off her nightgown.

She glanced at Aunt Grace, who was pulling her own things out of a dresser, and grinned to herself. The boys wouldn't think she looked at all like a witch if they could see her now; with her long hair all down instead of up in a tight bun and her nightgown nothing at all like the long black skirt she usually wore; it being all pink and frilly and all.

Esther finally got her long undergarments on, she stood up and pulled on her dress.

"Do you have boots?" Her aunt asked her, her voice sharp but not unkind.

"Yes, ma'am," Esther said and went over to her trunk.

She lost a few seconds because hanging above her trunk was a picture, one of a dozen Aunt Grace had in her room, which was of their mother and father, years earlier, just married. Her eyes teared up. They looked so wonderful.

She reluctantly pulled her eyes away from the picture, opened her trunk, and carefully pulled her clothes out until she arrived at the bottom, which was lined with shoes and books and pictures. She pulled out her work boots and put them on.

Her aunt frowned. "We will have to get you better boots for farm work. Those aren't nearly high enough."

Esther glanced at her aunt's boots which, indeed, were very high, coming almost to her knees. She could imagine that walking around in all of the muck of a farmyard would make high boots very useful. She would no doubt get water or mud in her own boots if she wasn't careful.

Esther followed her aunt out the door, with a last glance at Ruth, who was still sleeping, then down the very narrow stairs, through the very small front hall, and into a kitchen.

It wasn't a large kitchen, but it was very well-equipped. The stove was simply enormous, with six burners, four of which were very large. And it was all shiny metal. It must have cost a fortune. Hanging over it were all sorts of ladles and spoons, including several different sizes of slotted spoons.

And there were counters all around the room with almost nothing on them. Hanging from the ceiling above the solid wooden table were all sorts of pots and things, most of them huge... almost big enough to bathe Ruth in.

It was all painted in a very cheery yellow and very, very clean.

Aunt had stood and watched Esther as she looked around and then sharply said, "I will examine you to see what you know about cooking, but for this morning, I suppose you can manage oatmeal?"

"Yes, ma'am," Esther said, blushing. She could do a good deal more than that, although it would no doubt take her a while to get a handle on this new kitchen. Oatmeal was easy.

"Very well. The milk is downstairs in the cool room. You may set out anything that you see that you and your brothers like to eat. We have no shortage here. But we don't waste either, so be careful."

"Yes, ma'am," Esther said.

"Make sure you clean up after yourself here in the kitchen right away. If anything spills or boils over, wipe it up right away. We do not allow any messes here. When you have your sister in here, you will have to be very careful and teach her to be very careful as well."

"Yes, ma'am."

"The cool room door is down those stairs there," her aunt said, pointing to a door next to the one they had come in. "I will go upstairs and wake your brothers."

"I can wake them..."

"I said I will do it," her aunt said, even more sharply than usual. "I gave you your job."

"Yes, ma'am."

She watched her aunt stalk out of the kitchen and quickly went into the cool room. Then she realised that her aunt did not have gas lights and came back and lit a lantern.

The cool room was marvellous. It was every bit as clean as the kitchen, and the room she first walked into had lots of counters, just like the kitchen. Only these counters had pots and crocks and things on them, all covered up. The counters here weren't wood, like in the kitchen, but were all made out of some kind of stone.

She didn't want her aunt to catch her dawdling, so she looked around carefully till she saw a pitcher, and took the cloth off of the top to make sure it was milk. Esther moved the pitcher over to near the door where she wouldn't forget it, and then looked around for something else to serve for breakfast.

She had to lift the lids or cloths off several things, but eventually she found a ham with a large knife, both under a cover. Roger would be delirious if she served ham.

Esther ran back upstairs, found a plate, brought it down, placing it next to the ham. Then she, a bit nervously, took the knife and, very carefully, sliced off a few slices, which she put on the plate.

She looked around some more but seeing nothing else that she thought would go with their first breakfast, she carefully took the plate and the pitcher and walked upstairs, putting them down and going back for the lantern.

Then she went over to the stove and opened it. It was still hot, so she knew the coals were still lit, but it took a bit of work with a shovel to find them. Then she piled a few bits of kindling on them, and the kindling was just beginning to light when she heard noises on the stairs.

"Now, Roger," her aunt said, as she led her brothers into the kitchen, all dressed in their overalls, jackets, and what boots they had, "there is a stack of ordinary dishes that I hardly ever had call to use before but, now that you lot are here we will be needing daily. You take them down and wash them. They are in that cupboard over there..."

"Washing dishes is girls' work," Roger complained and, as quick as a wink, her aunt had him by the ear.

As she led a squealing Roger out the door, she said, "Robert, come with us to the woodshed."

His eyes wide, Robert followed his aunt out, carefully closing the door.

A few minutes later, Roger came back in, rubbing his backside. "She can give a licking," he said, grinning.

"What did she say?" Esther asked, and he paused in the middle of climbing on a chair to get the dishes out.

"She said as how if she gave Roger an order, then that was a 'Roger' job, and all I should care about is if it was a Roger job, and as how she'd have lots of boy work for me to do once I finished that. I stopped paying attention about then as she started on licking. She can lick."

Roger got the dishes down, and Esther spared them a glance. They were rather pretty dishes, white with a blue pattern of ducks and geese all around the edges. Several of them had small nicks, which must be why Aunt Grace regarded them as 'ordinary'.

They worked quietly for a couple of minutes, and then Robert came in, his arms full of wood. "Is that your job, then?" Esther asked.

"That is my responsibility, I'm told," Robert said, dropping the load into the wood barrel. "Gathering wood, chopping wood, chopping trees, bringing it in... everything to do with firewood which, she tells me, she needs a lot of for her cheese business, so I will be very busy."

"I don't know how to do all of that, but she says she'll teach me over the next couple of weeks."

Robert followed Aunt Grace inside, sore as anything. His hands were sore, his arms were sore, even his back felt sore from all of the bending over and picking wood up. Learning to chop wood was obviously not something that would happen in a day. Or maybe even a week.

"Robert!" Roger said, when he came in the door behind Aunt Grace, "Esther has cooked us up a feast! Oatmeal and ham!"

Esther blushed, and Robert grinned. He didn't think Roger did it on purpose, Roger hardly seemed to do anything on purpose, but he could be very effusive about food and Esther, who was sort of just learning to cook, always liked it. Even mother had always appreciated it. Robert tried to say complimentary things, but found it hard. He needed to learn to be better at complimenting people.

He took off his boots at the door and followed Roger and Esther through a door off the kitchen and into the next room. There was a table with several chairs around it and, in the middle of the table, a large pot of oatmeal, several large slices of fried ham beside it, and butter, salt, and brown sugar next to the oatmeal. Around that were set the ordinary plates that Aunt Grace had asked Roger to wash along with silverware.

"And a very nicely set table, too," his aunt said. "Let us sit down."

They had just started getting seated when they heard a wail from upstairs, and Esther gasped, "Ruth!" And ran off.

Roger stood looking at the table. "Can we eat?" he asked.

"Certainly not," his aunt said. "We will wait for Ruth and Esther."

"Yes, ma'am," Roger said.

Esther came back a few minutes later, holding Ruth, dressed. "I'm sorry it took me so long," she said, "it took me a while to find her clothes."

"Her seat is there, between us," Aunt Grace said, pointing to a chair with a booster on it that was next to herself, so Esther put Ruth down, then sat down herself on the other side, still holding Ruth's hand.

"Very well, now that we are ready, Robert, if you could pray for our meal."

Robert gulped, bowed his head, and repeated his father's meal prayer with a bit of a shaking voice.

Our Heavenly Father, kind and good,
We thank Thee for our daily food.
We thank Thee for Thy love and care.
Be with us, Lord, and hear our prayer.
Amen.

When he got done, he looked up, expecting people to give him funny looks, but no one said anything.

"And if you could serve us, please, Robert," his aunt said

into the silence.

He hastily stood up and, taking his aunt's bowl, ladled oatmeal into it. Then he reached for Roger's, which his brother was thrusting at him, but his aunt said, "Ladies first, Roger!" And Roger hastily pulled it back, waiting abashed while Robert served Esther and Ruth.

Aunt Grace had nodded at Esther, who, after a second or two, had started on the ham, cutting it into pieces and serving her aunt, her sister, then Roger, Robert, and finally herself.

After getting Esther started carving, Aunt Grace took the pitcher of milk and added some to her oatmeal. "I will have to show you where the cream is," she said, and Robert watched Esther's eyes widen.

"We, umm, we weren't able to use cream at home," he said. "I don't think we could afford it."

"Well, we certainly don't have that issue here. We own several cows which produce far, far more cream than we will ever use. So you should bring the cream to the table next time."

"Yes, ma'am," Esther said. "I saw it, but..."

"Yes, yes, I quite understand. Cream is expensive in cities. But not here. Cream, milk, cheese, clotted cream, as long as you are here you may eat all of it you wish. I put cream in all sorts of things... I make mashed potatoes with it, why, we can even have ice cream.

"Not," she added with a sharp tone and a glance at Roger, "that you may waste it. I expect everything set out to either be eaten or preserved for another meal."

"Yes, ma'am!" Roger said.

"Roger! Do not speak with your mouth full!"

Roger opened his mouth to reply, then nodded frantically and took another bit of ham. If he couldn't speak with his mouth full, he wouldn't be saying much at meals.

Esther, alone with Ruth in the kitchen, had frantically washed the dishes, afraid that at any moment her aunt would come back with the boys and be unhappy that the dishes weren't done. But when, the dishes finished, her aunt hadn't come back in, she had wandered all over the kitchen, then the dining room, then back down to the cool room, Ruth in tow, trying her best to memorise where everything was. Well, first to find it all, and then to memorise it.

Her aunt had a simply enormous stock of cheese! While Esther had been trying to memorise the cool room, Ruth had opened a side door and toddled in. Esther followed quickly to make sure there was nothing Ruth could break. But the room was filled with rack after rack of different kinds of cheese... some soft in tubs and some hard in wax covered wheels. Even Roger couldn't starve here. And, truthfully, Robert ate as much as Roger or even more. He just didn't talk about it all the time.

"Let's go back upstairs, Ruthy," she said, and as they walked up the cool room stairs, she heard the kitchen door open.

"Very good," she heard when she got to the top of the stairs and saw her aunt looking around the kitchen. "Now, I have told the boys it is time for us to go into the parlour."

Esther, a bit confused, followed her aunt into the parlour... which she hadn't yet examined. It was a very nice room, with one long couch and four padded, chairs. It had a small table in the centre, a short table that is, and on the walls...

"Books!" Roger said.

"Yes, books," Aunt Grace said. "Which is why we are

here. Now, Robert, you will be going first. Go to that shelf over there and take down the Bible. You will be responsible for reading our daily Bible lessons."

Robert, wide-eyed, went over and took down the Bible. "Sit next to me, and I will help you if you have any issues with any words," she said. "We are just starting out as a family, so we can start at the beginning. If you would read to us from Genesis chapter one, please."

After a bit of fumbling, Robert found his place and began reading. When he got to the sixth day, Aunt Grace stopped him. "That is quite enough, I think, for one lesson. Now set your mind to the text and tell us what you think God is telling us here."

Robert opened his mouth several times and then looked down at the page. "Well, umm... well, God made everything. So, I mean, it is important for us to do what He says because He made us."

"An excellent lesson," she said. "Now, Esther, on that shelf there are several cookbooks. Pick one that interests you and bring it over here."

Esther hurried over and looked, quickly deciding on "Savoury Pastry: Savoury Dish and Raised Pies, Pork Pies, Patties, Vol-au-vents, mincemeats and pies... by Vine, Frederick."[1]

She wasn't sure what the word 'savoury' meant, but it sounded good, and Roger liked pies.

"Very good, now you sit next to me," her aunt said, waving Robert away," and read to us. We will start at the beginning. Not the preface," she corrected when Esther turned to that page, "I'm sure no one was ever interested in prefaces. Turn to the first, well, it isn't a recipe, but we will read it anyway."

Esther turned and started reading a bit about what sort of butter was to be used in pastries and why. She read for about five minutes, and then her aunt said, "Very interesting. Now, Roger, you can read?"

"Yes!" Roger said quite indignantly.

"I thought your mother said as much," Aunt Grace replied calmly. "Now, I got in a stock of books just for you to read. They are on that shelf, over there, no, the lower one. I think you will like the first one, it is called..."

"Toby Tyler," Roger said, "Or ten weeks with a... with a..."

"Circus," his aunt said. "Now, come and sit next to me."

Roger took the book, and Esther quickly moved out of the seat next to Aunt Grace, which Roger reluctantly took.

But there was nothing at all reluctant about the way he read.

"TOBY'S INTRODUCTION TO THE ....CIRCUS"[2]

He read loudly and, except for the last word, quickly.

"Wouldn't you give more 'n,..."

"'N' isn't a word all by itself, is it?" he asked Aunt Grace.

"It's dialect, dear," she said, "It means 'more than', but the author wrote it as the boy might say it, 'More'n'."

Roger stared at the page, nodded, and went on.

"More'n six peanuts for a cent?" was a question asked by a very small boy, with big, staring eyes, of a candy vendor at a ... circus... booth. And as he spoke, he looked...

"What's that word?" Roger asked, pointing.

"Wistfully," Aunt Grace replied. "It means 'longingly' or 'with desire'... with hunger, in this case."

"Ah!" Said Roger.

"He looked wistely at the quantity of nuts piled high up on the basket, and then at the six, each of which now looked so small as he held them in his hand."

"Six what?" Roger asked.

"Six peanuts!" Robert said. "He already had six in his hand and wanted more, like you would."

Roger nodded vigorously

"Couldn't do it," was the reply of the proprietor of the booth, as he put the boy's penny carefully away in the drawer."

Roger continued to read quickly, eagerly, and with frequent questions and corrections. But everyone enjoyed it except Ruth, who had fallen asleep.

"Very well, now, I saw that you brought a book with you on the train. Is it of general interest, Roger?"

"Oh, yes, ma'am! It is a Henty about Holland and war and things."[3]

"Historical?"

"Yes, ma'am," Robert replied. "Henty is very accurate, historically."

"Then run and get it, Roger," she commanded, and he raced out of the door, clumped up the stairs, and was soon back, book in hand.

"Very well, now you can sit on the couch with your siblings, and I will read."

Aunt Grace opened the book, studied it for a few seconds, and then started...

THE "GOOD VENTURE"

Rotherhithe in the year of 1572 differed very widely from the Rotherhithe of today. It was then a scattered village, inhabited chiefly by a seafaring population. It was here that the captains of many of the ships that sailed from the port of London had their abode. Snug cottages with trim gardens lay thickly along the banks of the river, where their owners could sit and watch the vessels passing up and down or moored in the stream, and discourse with each other over the hedges as to the way in which they were handled, the smartness of their equipage, whence they had come, or where they were going. For the trade of London was comparatively small in those days, and the skippers as they chatted together could form a shrewd guess from the size and appearance of each ship as to the country with which she traded, or whether she was a coaster working the eastern or southern ports.

Most of the vessels, indeed, would be recognised and the captains known, and hats would be waved and welcomes or adieus shouted as the vessels passed...

The next half an hour was simply wonderful. Esther always loved Hentys, and Aunt Grace read them extremely well, putting in all of the excitement into exciting bits but without (as Roger did with his reading) getting too loud and distracting you.

Continuous effort - not strength or intelligence - is the key to unlocking our potential.

*— **Winston Churchill***

Chapter Three

THE YARD

"Very well, that is all for this morning. You have done the chores I have set you, I will set you more tomorrow, you can be sure, but growing children need play as well. You may go out and play. You may go in any direction, but be sure and come home when I ring the bell. You can see the bell on the kitchen shelf as you go out. It is a very large bell which I bought just to call you home."

Ruth had opened her eyes toward the end of the Henty, so all four of them trooped outside together. Robert was going to ask which way they should go when Roger suddenly darted out across a field and, without having any better direction, Robert and Esther, Ruth holding their hands, set out after him.

"Well?" Robert asked Esther.

"Well what?"

"How are you doing with the witch?"

"I don't think... oh, never mind. She isn't mother."

"No."

"But, well, I think it's going well."

"She's very strict. And demanding."

"But fair. Roger needed a licking this morning."

"Aye, that was a stupid thing of him to say. Father would have licked him for it."

"Especially if he said it to mother. Not that she is our mother," she hurried to say, "but... but she has all of the, the umm, the... there is a name for it. She's doing it, and so has... we need to respect her in that way."

"Yes. Well, I'm glad she isn't all, you know, touching and tender and all, like Aunt Lilly. Or any of the other aunts, really. All falling on your neck and saying she's sorry and all that. She is nice and cold, which is what I want, anyway. And Roger."

He looked at Esther, not sure if that was what she wanted. But she just nodded and then, "She... when she looks at me, she looks like she might cry. And she did cry last night, in bed. I think she thought I was asleep."

"Well, mother was her sister. You know they wrote all the time."

"Yes, but why does she cry when she looks at me?"

Robert looked at her. "You don't know?"

"No, why not at Ruth, or Roger... or..."

"You look like mother," Robert said. "None of the rest of us really do. Roger looks more like father and has his 'bounce' too. Ruth and I look like some mixture. But you look like mother. And I imagine you look very much like mother looked when she was..."

He broke off because Esther had turned away to cry.

"Hey, hey, hey!" He heard and saw Roger running back to them waving his hands. "Come this way! There's a creek!"

They turned a bit off to the left and, sure enough, there was a creek just inside a line of trees.

Roger quickly took his shoes and socks off, rolled up his pants and began dashing up and down the creek. "Roger!" Robert said, "Take them off! You are getting them wet." So

Roger went upstream, and a few seconds later, they heard him splashing even more dramatically.

"If you want to swim, too, that's OK," Esther said. "I might even take Ruth's shoes and stockings off and take her wading. It was cold this morning, but it has really warmed up now."

"No, I'll stay here with you. But feel free to wade up and down with her."

"Very well," she said, and a minute or two later, she led a squealing Ruth up and down the creek.

"Robert?" he heard a half an hour or so later and saw Roger poking his head around a tree, "I saw some fish. Do you suppose we can fish?"

"I imagine so," Robert replied, "but not today. We will have to make some fishing things."

"Doesn't Aunty have some?"

"I wouldn't think it likely," Robert replied. "A woman like that, down here fishing?"

"Probably likes fish as well as the next person."

"Probably trades cheese for them," Robert countered. "Esther told me she's got racks and racks of cheese."

"Really?"

"Yes. Now go off and swim some more before she calls us back."

Roger darted off, and Robert watched Esther. She was doing very well. She was doing very, very well with Ruth.

Robert hadn't been paying any attention at all to the sun, so he was shocked when he suddenly heard a loud bell. "Esther! Roger!" He shouted, jumping up. "It's the bell! We'll be late!"

Esther grabbed Ruth and raced up, frantically tugging on her socks. "Don't bother with Ruth," she said as Robert fruitlessly tried to pull her socks on. "I'll carry her; you carry her things."

Esther got her shoes on just as Roger came haring around the tree he had poked out from before, carrying his shoes and, Robert saw, wearing a rather wet shirt. As if it had been put on a very wet boy.

"Run, everyone," Robert said, and they pelted off toward the house, Roger darting off ahead as if hoping that he could avoid a licking by being first.

Robert held the door open for Esther and Ruth and went in himself, breathless. But, to his utter shock, his Aunt was not there, stick in hand, nor had she taken Roger off to the woodshed. Instead, she merely called, from the dining room, "Dinner is on the table."

They trooped in and, on seeing them, especially Roger, she said, "We will pray and then some of you had best go and put on dry clothes. Please put your wet clothes in the basket in the kitchen next to the oven, and I will deal with them later. Now, Robert, if you would please pray?"

They all stood behind their chairs, Esther still holding Ruth while Robert prayed. Then Roger darted out of the room while Esther got Ruth settled and then went off herself.

"I see you found the creek?" his aunt asked as Robert helped her to some sliced meat and mashed potatoes.

"Yes," Robert said, putting a slice of meat on his own plate and cutting it up for Ruth.

"That's good. Some of your chores will involve that creek. And I will expect you and Roger to routinely bring us fish when you have free time."

"Yes, ma'am," he said, watching her as she sprinkled some cheese on her potatoes... some crumbly white cheese.

Just then, Roger came racing in, pulled out his chair, sat down and, carefully observing that Ruth and Aunt Grace had their food, held out his plate, which Robert filled.

"Do you wish some cheese on your potatoes?" Aunt Grace asked him, holding out the bowl when he had his plate full.

He took it and looked at it. "Can I have butter?"

"Certainly. You can have both if you wish."

Roger stared curiously at the cheese, then shrugged his shoulders and, after a generous helping of butter (which mother would NEVER have allowed back home), put on an equally generous helping of cheese.

"It's good," he said, some seconds later, and then glanced at the look his aunt gave him and hurriedly swallowed. "It's very good, ma'am, the cheese and all. I've never had it on potatoes like this."

"Well, I always serve it that way," she said. "My husband liked it that way, and I grew accustomed."

Esther, when she sat down and Roger loudly told her of the custom, wrinkled her nose but, trying a small portion of the cheese, allowed it to be edible.

"We do not linger over dinner," Aunt Grace said a few minutes later. "We have a good deal of work to accomplish this afternoon."

At which Roger, who had been eating quickly, ate even more quickly, and Robert tried to take larger bites without anyone noticing.

"This afternoon," Aunt Grace said, rising from the table a few minutes later, "I will be introducing you... all of you... to barn chores. Yes, even Ruth. No, Esther, leave the table as it is. I will come back in and clear it once I have shown you each your chores."

Esther, wide-eyed, followed Aunt Grace and the others out the door. Robert knew why she was so surprised: leaving the table with food on it was simply not done back at their home.

"First of all," Aunt Grace said when they came in the barn

door, "Ruth will be our egg collector. Here, Ruth, take this basket."

Ruth reached out a hand and took the basket, staring curiously at it. "Here is where the chickens lay their eggs," Aunt Grace said, opening a small door and bending over to go in. "You will need to look all over, and when you find an egg, like this one, you put it very carefully in the basket."

So saying she left Ruth in the chicken coop and walked back out. "Now, Roger, it is good you are here. This barn is intended to have two layers of hay. One where the hay is all now," she pointed overhead, "and one way up there. I need for the hay to go to the upper loft. However, I am reluctant to climb that high. So what I need you to do..."

But Roger was already halfway up the ladder, and they all watched as he took an armful of hay and, rather awkwardly, climbed the next ladder with it.

"Very good. Now, Esther, you are next. Your job is simple, if a bit arduous. You will need to draw water for all of the animals. Each of them has a water trough, so it should be obvious enough how much they need. You will find a bucket by the door, and I hope you noticed the pump in the yard. From time to time, check on Ruth and, when she is done, keep her with you."

"Yes, ma'am," Esther said, turning to go outside.

"Now, Robert," Aunt Grace said, walking down an opening between several stalls while Robert, alone, followed her. "You will have the most difficult job. Each of you children will need to learn, but you will be the first. Learn to milk, that is."

Robert was alternately shocked and fascinated. He had always wondered where milk came from. He knew it came from cows, but...

"Now, this is a cow," Aunt Grace said. "When a cow is bred and has a calf, it comes into 'milk'. This is the same as for a human mother who has a baby. Her body gives off milk."

"Down here," she said, seating herself on a stool and indicating that Robert should sit on one beside her, "Are the cows 'teats'. That is what we call them. They are full of milk. The trick is getting it out and into the bucket. Watch closely."

Aunt Grace, having washed the teat and her hands, reached a hand out and, making a kind of 'O' with her thumb and forefinger, closed them around the top of the teat. Then she closed her other fingers, and a fine, strong stream of milk shot out and into the bucket. She did this three more times, then said, "Now, you try."

It certainly looked easy, but when Robert tried it the first time, nothing happened. "You need to squeeze tighter at the top," Aunt Grace said. "You are sending the milk back up into the cow."

He tried again and, this time managed a thin stream which shot out and wet the toe of his right boot. "Better," she said. "But you need to grip tighter."

And aim better, Robert said to himself and, after only a dozen more tries, got a halfway decent stream into the bucket. "Good. Keep going," Aunt Grace said, and got up. "I will milk the other one."

Aunt Grace moved to the other stall, and Robert soon heard rapid full streams of milk hitting her bucket. "As the man of the house, you deserve to know how we make our living," Aunt Grace said. "First of all, we make our money from our dairy."

"From these two cows?" Robert asked, surprised that she could earn a living from so little.

"No, we own five cows and one bull," she said. "We keep two cows here, three are with various neighbours. They bring me six gallons each week, one complete day's milking. The bull is in the south pasture. You lot should stay away from him. He is a rather friendly bull, but still dangerous. You will have to deal with him when we breed a cow or a neighbour brings a heifer or cow by to be bred. A heifer is a cow that has never had a calf."

"These cows each give six gallons a day?" Robert asked, looking at the paltry amount of milk at the bottom of his bucket.

"That's correct. Now even with you all here, I don't believe we will be drinking more than a gallon each day, or perhaps two. That will leave us ten or eleven gallons to use for our cheese business. Later I will take you into the cool room and show you how we make cheese and other milk products. And you will need to learn to help with the deliveries. Esther will be helping me with the dairy, as will Roger and Ruth when she gets big enough. But I think your time will be better spent on deliveries. With you here, we may be able to keep another cow at home.

"Yes, ma'am," Robert said. "I, umm, I'm not going to get to finish this very fast, I think."

"No one ever does their first time milking," she said.

"Now, in addition to the cheese business, and the various animals and crops we raise around the farm, my husband put aside three thousand dollars into very good securities, which produce a nice income of almost $150 every year... which I don't use, but have your Uncle Robert reinvest for me, so I now have almost four thousand dollars in the securities. All nicely 'diversified', your uncle tells me, which is what my husband said as well. It will be more expensive with you all living here, but I don't expect we will have to dip into our capital."

"Now, I will finish here, check on your siblings, and be back to finish off your cow. We don't want to make her wait too long."

Suddenly there was a thump from above them. "Well, Roger has learned how to get down from the upper loft," Aunt Grace said, looking up at the ceiling.

"I can tell him not to jump," Robert said.

"Don't be silly. Every boy that has ever moved hay has learned that he can get down faster by jumping."

Robert shook his head. He had thought she would be upset.

"It sounds like you are doing better," Aunt Grace said, getting up with her bucket and looking in at him. "A few days and you will be milking both of these by yourself, leaving me much more time to work on cheese and other products."

She stomped off... Aunt Grace was the loudest walker... and Robert held up his hands. They were getting sore!

Robert walked toward the back door, and Esther, who must have seen him coming, opened the kitchen door, so he just kept on walking with his bucket of milk, up the back stairs and into the kitchen, where he set it carefully down next to the others on the floor. All four children turned to Aunt Grace, wondering what they were to do next. "Very well, you have all done a very good job this afternoon you may go and play again. Come home when I ring the bell."

Robert picked Ruth up, and the four children streamed out of the kitchen; Robert, at least, was very pleased to get out of the house and out from under Aunt Grace's eyes. It seemed like his responsibility of 'firewood' was never-ending, and he also was learning to milk which, too, was going to be his responsibility, and everything had to be done just perfectly.

He didn't ask the others where they should go but just set off towards the driveway and then past it toward the nearby hill. It might be stupid, but although he was tired, he still felt like he wanted to do some serious walking.

He put Ruth down on the other side of a rail fence and climbed over. But when he picked her back up, she started to squirm, so he moved her to his shoulders. She seemed to enjoy that and kicked her feet lightly against his chest as she made noises that, he supposed, stood for various things she saw around her.

And it was a pretty walk. He slowed down a bit and looked at the scenery. The field they were climbing through was dotted with rocks. At the border stood some trees which he didn't recognise—tall trees with large leaves, with five points on them.

He heard Ruth squeal, looked where she was waving, and watched a rabbit bounce away. "Look, Roger, a rabbit," he said, turning, but Roger was still back by the fence, peering under some rock, probably watching ants. Roger loved ants. Roger loved pretty much everything that crawled along the ground or swam in a creek...

"Robert, wait up!" Esther said, and he saw her trudging along halfway between him and Roger.

"Tired?"

"Yes! I hate carrying all that water! My arms ache."

"Well, better not tell Aunt Grace," he said, turning to start up again. "She'll be all down on you for being lazy or something."

"Well..." Esther started to say, but Roger came running up, "Look, look at this beetle!"

Esther pulled away with a squeal, but Ruth's squeal was

very different. "Look, Ruthy," Roger said, holding the beetle up to her.

Robert noticed that she looked but didn't reach out for it. Indeed he didn't want to touch it. It was black with a shimmery green and had big black legs and pinchers that looked sharp.

Luckily Roger didn't ask him to take it but put it down and raced off to find something else interesting. Robert started after Esther, who had moved on up the hill when Roger had brought up the beetle.

"Oooh, look," Esther said a few minutes later. "A nest!"

It took Robert and Ruth a good deal of looking to see the nest, which was high in some tree in the crook between some branches. It was wonderful once they saw it, though, a big collection of sticks all woven together, three beaks peaking out over them and, from time to time, a bird flitting up to them and dropping something in one of the mouths.

They walked higher up the hill to a better spot for watching the birds and sat down. Ruth watched for a few minutes and then slid down off the rock he had put her on and began making piles of stones. Building something, no doubt.

Roger kept himself busy with insects, coming up every few minutes with some new beetle or worm and once even a really fuzzy caterpillar to show everyone.

Robert laid back. He never took naps, and the last few meals he had gotten to eat a simply enormous amount. He did his best to 'eat nice', but he ate a lot—nicely. And Roger simply stuffed himself. And Aunt Grace hadn't said anything!

But, anyway, he was kind of sleepy with all he had eaten and all the work she had him doing, so he lay back and alternated looking at the nest and closing his eyes...

And woke quite a while later, alone. "Roger?" he asked, sitting up.

"We're up here!" he heard Roger yell, and looked up the hill and saw Esther and Roger at, well, not the very top of the hill but a lot higher, sitting on a rock. "Come look!" Roger yelled.

Robert sighed. He didn't really want to do all that much more climbing. But he didn't want to be a spoilsport either. "What is it?" he asked when he finally reached the others, where he saw Ruth laying at their feet.

"Look what you can see!" Roger said, waving his arm over the valley.

Robert turned, and it was pretty amazing. He couldn't see his Aunt's house, but he could see most of the road they had taken, the railway station, and a train chugging its way away from it. "Awesome," he said.

The three of them continued to sit, and Roger and Esther continued to comment on the wildlife, but Robert just stared at the trees which hid Aunt Grace's farm from view.

He wanted his old life back, but he knew that was impossible. He wanted to cry, scream, or sit in a corner and mope, but everything his father had always taught him assured him that he had to act in the right way regardless of his own feelings. "Gird up your loins, Boy!" his father would say, often with a cuff to his head, whenever Robert would pause, hesitate, or start crying when something needed to be done.

And now he was glad for every cuff. He couldn't imagine how disappointed his father would be if he had let down his siblings just when they needed him the most.

"I think we need to go now," Esther said.

"I didn't hear the bell," Roger said, darting off to watch a black squirrel that was shaking its tail vigorously in a nearby tree.

Robert looked down at Ruth at Esther's feet. "Let's wait a little while until she wakes up. I don't want to carry her."

"I can carry her," Esther said a bit doubtfully.

"Down this hill," Robert asked. "I don't think so. Let's just wait a while."

It turned out to be a long time before she woke, and Roger insisted on darting off after everything he saw, so it was quite a while later when they arrived back at the house.

Aunt Grace was standing in the kitchen when they arrived, and Robert did not like the look on her face. Even less did he like what she said, "Robert, if you would join me in the woodshed, please."

When she finished, she looked very earnestly at Robert, who was doing his best not to cry and largely failing. "When you are with your siblings, you are in charge. You heard my instructions; they were the same as I have given each time. I told you clearly to come back when I rang the bell."

"We didn't hear the bell," Robert sobbed.

"Well, then, it was your responsibility to see that you were where you could hear it. Life on a farm involves many very serious responsibilities. Animals, and even people, might die if you do not take them seriously."

"And make no mistake, Robert, I will apply the same standard to Esther and even Roger. When they are in charge, they are the ones I will punish."

"But what if they won't come?"

"Is that what happened here?" she asked, her face harsh.

"No," Robert admitted, "But what if?"

"Then you will need to discipline them. You were in charge, Robert."

"Yes, ma'am."

Roger shovelled in the wonderful meat and marvellous potatoes, drank another glass of milk, which he'd never had so much of in his whole life, and watched Aunt Grace the whole time out of the corner of his eyes. But while she kept rescuing Ruth from spilling her milk, she didn't say a word to Roger or even give him a funny look, no matter how much he ate. He tried to be careful about the way he ate so maybe she wouldn't even notice how much he was eating.

Esther noticed, and had given him a couple of quick frowns, but mostly she just kept chatting with Aunt Grace.

Eventually, he couldn't hold any more and, making sure to scrape his plate very clean and get the last little bit of gravy, he sat back.

"We will have dessert later," Aunt Grace said as if she had been watching him. "But now we will clear our plates and go into the parlour."

Roger hopped up with the others and grabbed his plate. "Don't forget your silverware, Roger," Esther said, and he quick piled his silverware onto his plate and followed them into the kitchen, where there was a bucket with some water. He had to get the food bits off and stack everything in the sink.

"Very well, now let us go into the parlour."

Roger followed, wondering if he was going to get to read out loud again. He had liked that.

"We will be spending the evenings in the parlour," Aunt Grace said. "Esther, you keep an eye on Ruth, and when she looks tired, you can take her up and put her down. Now I have bought you each a journal," she went on, going over to the bookcase. "You can write in it, draw in it, or even press flowers or..." she looked at Roger, "...pin bugs, as long as you do it carefully. There is information on how to do so in that natural encyclopaedia."

"You may also read books, but not the books we are reading for story time, well, except for the Bible. You may always read that. I will expect this to be a quiet time where you prepare yourself for bed. Indeed you may dress for bed whenever you wish."

Esther gave Ruth a book, and then she and Robert both picked up their journals, but Roger went to the bookshelf and started looking. This was joy. Especially since she had said they were going to have dessert later.

Roger found a book by L. Frank Baum, not one of the Wizard series, and started looking at it. He read for a while, then glanced at Robert, who was drawing pictures of trains, and then looking at the bookshelf as if he would rather be getting a book. It wasn't like Aunt Grace told them they had to write in their journal!

He heard steps and looked up to see Aunt Grace coming in with... he got up and went over and looked as she put it down on the table... something with cherries and brown stuff and... "It's a cherry cobbler, Roger. You will like it, I'm sure."

Roger's hand darted out toward the big spoon that Aunt Grace had brought and froze at her look. "May I serve everyone, ma'am?" he asked.

"You certainly may," she answered, smiling at him as if she knew full well he had been intending to take his own portion. "I'll bring the cream."

Roger, his mind whirling at the idea of getting to put cream on an already luxurious desert, carefully scooped out four portions into four bowls, doing his best to make them all as even as he could, so that no matter which bowls the others took he would still get a full serving. Then he scooped another portion, smaller, for Ruth.

Aunt Grace came in just as he finished with a small pitcher. "I think I will serve the cream, Roger," she said. "It can be a bit tricky. Esther? Would you like cream on your cobbler?"

"Yes, please," Esther replied, coming over and taking a bowl and spoon after Aunt Grace had poured the cream.

Robert got cream, too, and Roger got his next and took it over to his chair, where he did his best to read his book and eat his dessert at the same time without spilling anything. Unsuccessfully.

"Roger!"

"Yes, ma'am. I'll go get a napkin," he said and hurried off to the kitchen.

The next time he looked up from his book Esther and Ruth were gone and Robert and Aunt Grace were both reading.

Roger was too tired to read anymore and did not want Aunt Grace telling him that he had to go to bed, so he quietly got up, put his book carefully back on the shelf, and took his dishes to the kitchen where he quietly rinsed them in the bucket. He didn't want his aunt calling him back because he had forgotten something.

Upstairs, his nightshirt on, his prayers said, he rolled up in his blanket on his wonderful new bed. Roger spent a few moments where his eyes were insisting on crying, but he soon had his thoughts all focused on all of the wonderful things that he would get to do tomorrow, and, the wind gently blowing a branch against the wall near their window, he fell asleep.

There are three great truths, 1st, That there is a God; 2nd, That He has spoken to us in the Bible; 3rd, That He means what He says.
— Hudson Taylor

Chapter Four

THE CHURCH

"Boys, you may go and play when you finish here," Aunt Grace said loudly from the stall where she was milking. "Esther, come in the house when you are done."

"Where do you want to go?" Roger asked Robert, leaning down from the loft.

"Let's go upstream this time," Robert said.

A few minutes later, the boys reached the creek uphill of the farm. Robert took his clothes off and hung them up from a limb, and Roger, seeing him, shucked his too and soon the boys were wading up the creek. The water was freezing, and the stones hurt his feet, but Robert was glad to be in the water, anything to take his mind off...

"Look, Robert," Roger said, jumping almost in a dive into a deeper part of the water and splashing furiously to keep himself from being washed back down with the flow. "It's deep enough to swim!"

Robert walked up and watched his brother alternately jump wildly in and get washed back.

How did Roger do it? It was like he didn't even care that

their parents were dead. That they had to come and live with their crazy aunt.

Poor Esther, she even had to sleep in the same bed as Aunt Grace. And she was now going to be all afternoon working with her, learning to make cheese.

He suddenly panicked. Were they too far away?

He turned and looked through the trees. No. He could see the farm. They would easily hear the bell from here.

"Look, Robert, a duck!"

Robert looked, but Roger's yell had startled the poor bird, and all Robert saw was a flurry of brown wings.

"If you were quieter, I would have gotten to see it," Robert complained.

"If I had been quieter, you wouldn't have listened," Roger responded. "Wonder what's for dinner?"

Robert gritted his teeth. All Roger seemed to be able to talk about was food!

After a few seconds of silence, Roger said, "I wonder when I'm going to get to learn to milk?"

"Soon, I hope," Robert said. "It's hard! I could use some help."

"Well, I've got most of the hay up top, so I guess I'll get a new job soon. Aunty said I could feed the pigs. Only she said we didn't hardly have any scraps with me here," Roger added, grinning.

Robert almost opened his mouth to yell at Roger but closed it just in time. Why did he want Roger to be miserable? It wouldn't help anyone!

He went over and tried diving in the water. Oh, it was cold, and too shallow, but at least it kept his mind off... everything. And going under the water like this kept Roger from talking to him. Not that that bothered Roger, who was looking at some nest near the water's edge.

"Let's keep going upstream!" Roger said a few minutes later.

"OK, but not too much further; we need to hear the bell."

Roger grinned, "You do, anyway. Or you'll get licked."

"Oh, and if I run home when the bell rings and tell Aunt Grace that you wouldn't come."

Roger's smile slipped a bit. "Let's not try it."

"Good idea. But we can still go up a ways."

"Oh, look, Robert, a fish!"

Robert looked, and there was a very nice trout... indeed, several trout.

"Run back to the house and get the fishing things," Robert said. "Maybe we can bring some home. Carpe diem, as father would have said."

"You mean Carpe fishem," Roger responded but then ran off.

It was several minutes later when he came back with the net and poles and all. Robert had dug around while he was gone and had found a few worms, so he quickly put a worm on one hook and dangled it into the water.

"You got one!" Roger said, dancing from foot to foot, watching.

"Yeah, now grab me the keeper string..."

Roger had the line in, and Robert was looking at a bush which was practically drowning in a vine, when they heard the bell. Roger quickly pulled his line out of the water and wound it up, but Robert stared through the trees at Aunt Grace, who stood swinging the bell up and down violently. It was a very loud bell; he didn't really have any excuse for not hearing it the first time. They had gone much too far and been gone much too long.

He turned back and pulled on his clothes and then he and Roger went back to the house.

They arrived back in the kitchen, Roger proudly holding

up their keeper string, which had four gutted fish on it, to Esther, alone, standing by a stove which had several large pots of water on it. And a delightful smell.

"Look what we got! What's cooking?" Roger said.

"Right now, bathwater," Esther said, taking the string from him. "Dinner is laid out in the dining room. We have already fed and bathed Ruth, and she is upstairs in her bed. You two go and eat. I'll put these downstairs."

Roger followed Robert into the dining room, where bread, butter, ham, cheese, milk, and mustard were laid out at the table. "Umm, I guess I should pray," Robert said as Roger moved eagerly to the table. Seconds later, Roger was helping himself to an enormous sandwich that he had made. Esther came in.

"Aunt Grace and I will be bathing," she said, looking very tired. "Then it will be your turn. Robert, please make sure that Roger gets his water, and gets himself clean. And please turn the intake for the stove all the way down before you go to bed. Oh, and I'll be back after my bath to put the food away."

Roger stared after her. "Why baths?" he asked, taking a bite.

"Tomorrow's Sunday," Robert answered. "Church." Robert grinned at Roger, who was making a bit of a face. Roger hated sitting still in church, but he liked playing with the other boys before and after.

"Don't want a bath," Roger said, finally.

"Well, you'll have one whether you like it or not. I don't want a licking because you were dirty behind the ears. Aunt Grace'll likely check."

Robert yawned. Aunt Grace had gotten them up early on Sunday, and he had done almost all of the milking, and Roger had done most of Esther's chores while the girls 'got ready.' It had been hard waking up so early, and he wasn't exactly thrilled to be going off to church and having to meet all sorts of new people and all, but mostly he was just tired from getting up so early.

Roger was driving, which kept him awake and excited. It was basically the road back toward the train station, only they had passed the train station and continued into town—and Roger was very excited to be driving.

"The church is the last building on the left, Roger," Aunt Grace said. "I will park the buggy when we get there, as the yard can get rather crowded."

She took over the reins just as they passed a large white house on the right-hand side of the street and turned them to the left, into a well-used yard.

"Robert, if you and Roger would get out the dutch ovens under the seat, please," Aunt Grace said as they got down from the buggy. "Esther and Ruth, come with me. Boys, bring the ovens around to the front of the church.

Roger and Robert turned to the front of the buggy as the girls walked off, and Robert saw a pile of blankets under the front seat. "There's three of them!" he said, staring at the ovens that had been under the blankets.

Roger jumped up and looked. "They look heavy!"

"I'll slide this one to the edge, do you get down, and we'll take it together."

The two boys walked carefully, each of them leaning out away from the other, carrying the heavy Dutch oven between them. "Oh, good," Esther said, hurrying up. "Over here, I have reserved room by this fire."

"You knew we had these?" Robert asked.

"Didn't I? What did you think I did all yesterday after-noon while you two were off fishing?"

"What's in them?" Roger asked, reaching for the lid.

Esther slapped him, "You'll see. Now go get the other two. They need to warm up, or they won't be nearly as good."

That encouraged Roger, and he hurried, getting to the buggy and sliding the next one to the edge before Robert arrived.

Esther looked at the dutch ovens sitting by the fire, couldn't figure out any further excuse to stay out here, so took Ruth's hand, very glad that she got to be a 'big sister'. Somehow that made the task of facing this new church less daunting. She had seen several other girls, mostly bigger, moving their own dutch ovens and the like, but hadn't spoken to any of them. They were all wearing actual church dresses...

Well, not that girl! A girl had come running down a trail, not in a wagon or anything, and she had on a, well, it was hardly even a work dress. And she had bare feet. At church?

They mounted the steps and had to wait behind a rather portly woman who was greeting the pastor. Esther reached up and adjusted her head covering, which was always slipping to one side.

"Well, good morning," the pastor said to Esther when it was their turn. "You are...?"

"I am Esther, and this is Ruth," Esther said. "We're staying with Mrs Livingston."

"I thought that might be who you were. And you were helping with the food, quite good of you. Your aunt's pew is toward the front on the left."

"Thank you," she said, and pulled Ruth down the aisle.

The line moved very slowly, so she had time to look at all of the people. That girl wasn't the only one not in church clothes. There were two families, both sitting in the middle of the church, who wore their work clothes, and the boys were all barefoot as well.

She and Ruth finally got to the pew where Aunt Grace was sitting. Several children who had been sitting there all scooted quickly over at the look Aunt Grace gave them, one of them getting on an older boy's lap.

Esther sat down and gathered Ruth onto her lap so there would be room for Roger and Robert when they came, and started looking around. She began feeling a bit better about her dress. It wouldn't have done at all for town, but it wasn't that bad here. Several other girls had dresses of the same material as Esther's; and that one poor girl, who she saw sitting with her whole family together in a row... they were all very shabbily dressed. But they looked very happy.

Robert, with Roger close behind him, hurried over to the line going into the church. It was a very pretty country-style church, with whitewashed walls and a tall steeple with a bell still ringing. The planks were put together tongue and groove, which Robert had thought really amazing when his father had taught him about them.

"Look, Robert, look at the horses," Roger said, elbowing Robert, as a nice set of grey horses came into the yard, a man driving beside a woman with four children in the back of the wagon.

"I bet he's the banker," Robert whispered back, seeing how nicely the man was dressed.

"Lots of kids," Roger said.

There did seem to be quite a few children at this

church...but maybe it was because they all were coming in at the same time, a bit late.

They were greeted by the pastor at the door, but Robert's eyes were on the doorframe, which was very well done. He had to grip Roger's hand to prevent him from going and sitting with another boy in the back of the church. What would Aunt Grace think of that? She would probably come right back and get him—right in the middle of church.

They were the last two in their pew, which was a bit tight. Roger immediately grabbed the Psalter out of the back of the pew in front of them. He saw Aunt Grace glance at Roger, but she didn't say anything, so Robert didn't take the Psalter away. If Roger would get distracted, a Psalter was a good distraction.

There was a very short stage, with four chairs and a pulpit. Very plain, all made with rough, unfinished wood. Well, except for the pulpit, which was all varnished and everything.

But the building was very nicely done for a country church. The walls and ceiling were all made of wood which meant that you could hear the slightest sound, which would be good for singing.

The pastor walked to the front, but it was another man who stood up with a Psalter and said, "Psalm 83".

Robert looked around, but there was no piano! The man just hummed a couple of notes, and everyone started singing. The man behind them had a wonderful bass voice, and Roger spun around to watch him. Robert saw Aunt Grace frown and elbow Roger, who spun around and began to sing lustily... if not exactly in tune.

No one commented, though, even when Roger missed a couple of words. Indeed probably no one could hear him except Robert and the fat lady sitting in front of them;

everyone was singing so lustily. Even Aunt Grace, who sang the alto with a bit of nasal.

And they sang eight whole Psalms! At their church in town they never did more than three, with one more at the end.

The singing and the Bible reading done, everyone sat down, and the preacher began preaching. His text was the book of Nahum, which Robert had seldom heard of, but Robert wasn't paying good attention. He was looking at the wonderful old beams holding up the ceiling. Or, he supposed, the roof? The boards were all above the beams, and the roof must be directly above them... they couldn't be the roof itself, but they were just together...

An hour or so later, he was shocked to see everyone standing up, and he quickly stood up with them.

"Oh, Lord, we thank you for this wonderful day to gather and worship you. We thank you for your wonderful grace exercised in judgment, as we see in this book of Nahum. And Lord, we thank you especially for the four new young people which you have brought to us through the midst of tragedy..."

Robert suddenly realised that the pastor was speaking about them! His ears burning, he waited desperately for the 'Amen' and turned... but they were at the front of the church, and everyone was standing around and greeting... and Aunt Grace, who didn't seem too comfortable herself, was having all sorts of people, including the preacher and his wife, gathering around and talking about how wonderful she was and how were the new orphans doing...

"Robert!" Roger was tugging on his arm and pointing to a side door right at the front of the church.

Robert quickly glanced at Aunt Grace, but she was surrounded and wouldn't notice... so followed by Roger and his sisters, he ducked out the side door.

Esther picked Ruth up and followed Robert and Roger out the door, glad to be out of the sanctuary and all of the 'orphan' comments. They found themselves alone in a side yard with some scattered trees a few yards away. Right next to the church were flower boxes filled with bright red and yellow flowers. The boxes were just the right height to sit on and had benches all along them.

They hadn't been there long when two other children, young girls, came out that same side door, ran over to a large box at the end of the field, and pulled out some jump ropes. Esther noticed them giving her glances, but she wasn't quite ready to go play. Not after that prayer! She had never been so embarrassed in all her life.

Four boys came around the corner from the front door and went over to the trees, where they climbed up and started hanging from their legs. Esther grinned. The boy's shirts kept flopping down over their faces, so they had to let go with one hand and push the shirt back with the other. One boy didn't get his grip quite right and fell down, but he just dusted himself off and climbed back up with a grin.

Four more girls, two of them quite a bit older, came out and took a longer jump rope from the box, the two older girls starting it swinging for the smaller girls. Esther was trying to work up the courage to take Ruth over there when she heard a loud voice behind her.

"And who are you?" It was a boy about Robert's age coming up to them, followed by three younger boys and a girl. The older boy was wearing a very nice Sunday suit, nicer than almost any she had ever seen.

"My name is Robert," Robert said, holding out his hand.

"Bob, eh?" The boy said, ignoring the proffered hand. "And all of these are your siblings? All following you like little ducklings? I think we will call you Bob and the Bobtails. No, just 'The Bobtails'. That goes well, I think?"

He glanced at the children standing with him, but they didn't say anything.

"Do you all have names?" The boy came up to Roger and looked him in the face.

"None your business," Roger said, and darted off to where a group of younger boys were climbing a tree and hanging from their legs.

"Little ruffian," the boy said, and turned to Esther. "And you?"

"My name is Esther," she said. "We are..."

"We all know who you are," the boy said, "stray orphans that Mrs Livingston picked up. And who is this one with her hand in her mouth?" he said, bending down to stare at Ruth. "Is she too ignorant to speak? Or can she pronounce her own name?"

"Master Trenton!" Esther heard, and jumped. The boy himself looked shocked, and they both turned to see Aunt Grace, only a few yards away, obviously having heard the whole exchange.

"Yes, ma'am?" the boy said, his voice quavering.

"If I could see you in the woodshed, please, Master Trenton?"

He turned white. "Yes, ma'am," he said, and, to Esther's shock, turned to go.

"My name is Lilly," the girl said, coming over. "This is your sister?"

"Yes, her name is Ruth."

"We're all so sorry," the girl said. "Father prayed for you last week too, right from the pulpit."

"Thank you," Esther said, her eyes still on the boy. "He went with her?"

"Oh, yes. Oh, yes, he had to. Father... he's my brother... father doesn't lick us much, but he would get double lickings if he didn't go. Mother will be upset, but..." she giggled, "she won't say anything to Mrs Livingston. She would to anyone else; she always stands up for him—but not to Mrs Livingston."

They heard cries coming from the woodshed. "She tried— once. It was right after Mrs Livingston had been appointed Sunday school Superintendent. She was visiting the boy's class when Geoffrey, that's his name, said something to the teacher."

"She called him out and he told mother. Mother confronted her right in the yard and asked her what her son had done that meant he needed a licking."

"Well, Mrs Livingston called Geoffrey over, right in front of everyone, and asked him if he would like to tell his moth- er... and father had come over by then, but she didn't mention him... if he would like to tell his mother what he had done, that meant he needed a licking."

"Well, Geoffrey had told mother he had 'done nothing,' but he knew that wouldn't work in front of everyone, so he just said he'd rather not."

"So Mrs Livingston, your Aunt Grace, just turned to mother and said that if she wished to know, she could ask him. Which mother didn't do, as she knew full well that Geoffrey must have done something bad, which now every- body knew, so she just left it."

Robert stood very awkwardly as Geoffrey hollered in the woodshed. Why was that boy so nasty?

Roger seemed to be playing well, but no one else came to greet Robert and... and he hated this kind of thing. He hated being new and trying to make friends. And there didn't seem to be anyone else his age, really. Besides the boy, which, thankfully, had stopped hollering.

Roger came running back but didn't say anything, just standing by Robert's side, and then Robert noticed that pretty much all of the boys except the very littlest were wandering off, all in the same direction. Robert followed them, with Roger tagging along. They went to a shed at the side of the church, one of them opened it, and they were soon handing tables out. Robert grabbed one side of a table as it came out, and Roger hurried up to take the other side. They had no idea where the other boys were going so they just followed them around the side of the church and soon saw that they were setting them out in the yard.

They set a dozen or so tables out, and then they all started hauling benches, which they set up all around the tables. It was funny; there weren't any adults telling them what to do. He guessed the boys were just all used to doing it.

A loud bell rang as Esther and Lilly sat talking in the yard after church, and Lilly started running. "Come, Esther," she said. "That's the meal bell."

All the other children were running, and Esther, dragging Ruth, had a hard time keeping up with Lilly. As soon as they got around the corner, they stopped, as the other children in front of them had stopped, and Esther looked around, surprised.

Since church had let out, someone had brought out a whole bunch of tables with benches around them. Most of the tables were set to sit at, but at the front were three other tables with no benches; but all of the food. Esther noticed Aunty's dutch ovens, and Aunty, and lots of other women, were standing around the head table fussing with the food, and the men were all walking in from the other side of the church.

"Your aunt can cook!" Lilly said to Esther as the girls moved closer to the tables and stood waiting for the preacher to say a prayer.

"I know it! I was there all afternoon yesterday when we made it. Does she always make so much?"

"Oh, yes. You always want her to come to your parties because she will bring ever so much savoury food."

"What's savoury food?" Esther asked. She hadn't yet figured it out from her reading.

"Like... meat and things, not pies and cakes and cookies. She hardly ever makes them. And she almost always makes something with milk or cheese...?" Lilly said, giving Esther an enquiring glance.

"Oh, yes. Milk and cheese and potatoes and onions..."

"Oh, I love that! We'll have to get in line quick to get some."

"We made three whole dutch ovens of it... Oh, the preacher."

Everyone bowed their heads, and the preacher prayed pretty quickly. Then Lilly pulled her off to the line.

"We made three whole dutch ovens of it," Esther protested, taking two plates while Ruth watched curiously.

"Oh, she always does. But it always goes so quickly. I don't think she ever takes any of it home."

Esther grabbed some sliced ham and some corn in the line, and then helped herself to a spoonful of Aunt Grace's potatoes. She kept going down the line. Someone had made some kind of pie with chocolate in it that looked interesting. And there were several kinds of pickles, so she took some of each.

"What did your mother make?" She asked Lilly when she sat down, tasting a pickle and wrinkling her nose. This pickle was spicy!

"Oh, the corn," Lilly said, reddening slightly. As well she might, there hadn't been much corn in the line. Why Aunt Grace had brought three whole dutch ovens of the potatoes!

"The corn is very good," Esther said, quickly taking a bite.

"Yes, I like it too. I helped her put it up at harvest. One of the men brought it over as his tithe, a whole bunch of it, and we put it all up very quickly, except what we ate. Oh, we worked so hard. Even Geoffrey."

Esther giggled at the idea of Geoffrey putting up corn. The way he dressed for church it looked like he never could do any work or he would get his clothes all mussy.

Water would certainly wet us, as fire would certainly burn...
— **Rudyard Kipling**

Chapter Five

THE SWIMMING HOLE

"Robert?"

Robert looked up from the back of the buggy. Roger had been driving but, he saw, they had pulled over and Roger was getting down.

"The boy's swimming hole is over there," Aunt Grace was saying. "I understand that it is a favourite Sunday activity for the boys here, and it is important that you get to know them. Not all of the boys in our town go to our church, and many boys don't go to your school either. There are three other small schools in the area of our town. But I understand... I've never been, obviously... that most of them come here for swimming on Sunday when the day is even close to warm enough.

"It is too far from our house for you to easily hear the bell, so please be back... no, please leave by sunset. We will hold supper until you get there."

Robert climbed down. He loved swimming but wasn't thrilled with the idea of having to meet however many boys would be there.

Roger, on the other hand, raced off in the direction Aunt

Grace had pointed. Robert saw him get to the tree line, stop, listen, turn to his right, race off that direction, and then turn down a path.

When Robert got near the tree line, he heard what Roger had heard, a bunch of boys yelling and several loud splashes. But he couldn't see anything; the underbrush was too thick.

A few yards further, he stopped and stared because in front of him was a creek, just a couple of yards wide, which then opened out into the swimming hole. And beside him, strung on a dozen branches, were several dozen sets of clothes and shoes and all.

As he undressed and hung up his clothes, he stared at the swimming hole. It seemed like it had about an acre of water in an enormous 'S' shape, and, just to his left, the creek fell down into it with a little waterfall. And, on the far side, was a huge oak tree with one branch that went practically horizontal several yards out into the hole and was covered with young boys jumping or diving off. Indeed most of the pool was surrounded by trees, making practically the whole thing be in the shade except the very middle.

He went over the little rise and almost stumbled on a very Little Boy, about Ruth's age, who was splashing about in the mud at the edge of the water. Several older boys lay on the grass on the edge of the bank, some of them keeping an eye on the toddler and several of his fellows.

But the boys near Robert's age seemed to mostly be swimming in the deep part of the pond, so he splashed in the water and gasped. This water was cold!

He noticed one of the older boys looking at him and grinning, so, gritting his teeth, he made a shallow dive in the direction of the other boys. Freezing!

Roger loved this limb. It was just high enough for him to jump from without feeling scared, and high enough for him and the other boys to make a big splash.

Roger was with several other boys his age, jumping off the limb. They were making a lot of noise, but not talking. Robert was swimming in the middle of the pond, mostly alone, along with several other boys more his age. A few older boys were sitting mostly on the bank, talking. Probably about girls.

Roger noticed a new boy come running up and frowned. It was that nasty boy, Geoffrey, the preacher's kid, who wore the fancy clothes... which he was taking off.

"Hey, Bobtail!" He yelled, splashing into the water toward Robert.

Roger missed the next bit as it was his turn to jump off the limb, but when he got up on it again, Robert and Geoffrey were standing on the bank, with a group of other boys standing around them, and Roger was shocked to see Geoffrey strike Robert! Right in the face!

Roger stood on the limb to watch, as did several other boys. Robert had gone back a bit when he'd gotten hit but then rushed forward and sunk his head into Geoffrey's chest, sending them both to the ground... the mud.

Roger grinned as Geoffrey pulled himself out of the mud, and before he really had gotten up, Robert had landed on him again, swinging out. But Geoffrey landed a blow on Robert's face which knocked him back and gave Geoffrey time to get up.

Geoffrey landed one more blow before Robert, again, rushed at him and, this time, butted him in the stomach. They both landed in the edge of the pool, where the deep mud met the water.

Two of the bigger boys slowly got up and went forward, grabbing Robert and Geoffrey, who were still struggling together in the mud. "All right, you two!" One of the bigger boys said, swatting at Robert, who swung out at him. "Good fight and all, time to be done; we need our rest. Shake and break."

Geoffrey looked as if he wouldn't shake, but the boy holding him pinched his upper arm and, after squealing, he held out his hand, and the two boys went off in different directions, Robert coming over to the limb.

"You got him good!" Roger said as Robert climbed up, several smaller boys coming to look.

"He got me good!" Robert said, fingering his eyes. "What will Aunt Grace say?"

"You're going to have a good shiner," Carl, one of the boys from church who had been on the tree with Roger, said, looking at Robert's eyes.

"He can hit!" Robert said. "He didn't seem to want to fight at church."

"Doesn't like to get his clothes mussy," Carl said. "He won't hardly ever fight with them on. He's ever a one for nice clothes, Geoffrey. More than mother, even."

Robert looked at him, "He's your brother?"

"Yup. Oldest brother."

"Does he always pick on the new kids?"

Carl paused in thought, "We ain't never had new kids before, so I can't tell. He doesn't get along well with others, though. Teacher often says so, and Father is ever lecturing him on it."

"Well!" Robert said, looking over at where Geoffrey was sitting with a couple of bigger boys.

"Are they friends?"

"Geoffrey ain't really friends with anyone," Carl said. "But he and that boy get along OK, I guess."

"What grade is he in?" Roger asked Carl.

"Oh, he ain't in school no more," Carl said. "None them bigger boys are... gotta call them men now, I suppose. They all done dropped out or graduated or whatever. Geoffrey is the biggest boy left. Fathers need their boys to help on the farm or whatever. George, there, his father is at the store, and George does supply runs and all, been doing them for two years. I think that's a fun job, getting to haul stuff all day on the wagon. Sit there, drive through the countryside."

"He just quit school to go full-time with the wagon about two weeks ago. He kept being late or missing days before that anyway, so his folks decided he should just drop school. He's going to do some evenings with my dad, I reckon. That made Geoffrey the oldest boy in school, which he complained of... but I think he was kinda glad. And then you came along!" he said, grinning at Robert. "Oh, was he mad! Which is stupid, but Geoffrey is real smart but not very bright."

Which Roger thought was a funny thing to say. How could he be smart but not bright?

Esther was in the kitchen getting a glass of milk for Ruth when the boys walked into the kitchen door. She gasped, "Robert? What happened?"

"Geoffrey," Robert said.

"You should have seen it, Esther! They scrapped and scrapped! Geoffrey got him in the eye, which you see, and then..."

"Shush," Robert said, cuffing him lightly on the back of the head. "We don't want Aunt Grace to find out."

"Well, I don't see how she can miss it!" Esther said. "With that eye and all. Well, nothing for it. She's waiting for us in the parlour. Supper will be ready in about half an hour; we weren't sure when you would come in, so she says for us to start our evening reading now, and we'll eat then."

She took the milk and went into the parlour where, a few minutes later, the boys came in: Roger going straight to the bookshelf and Robert walking there more slowly.

Esther watched Aunt Grace closely. She looked up from her own book, some book of poetry, and saw Robert, and grinned!

"Have a good time at the swimming hole?" she asked.

Robert didn't say anything, but Roger filled in the gap. "Sure did! Did you know they have this big limb which hangs out over the water? All of us boys would climb up on it, walk out over the water, and then jump in. Some of them even dove, which I haven't really learned to yet."

"You should ask a bigger boy to teach you," Aunt Grace said.

"Robert knows how," Roger said. "I'll get him to teach me."

"Wasn't the water cold?" Esther asked.

"When you first get in," Robert said. "You warm up quickly."

"You seemed to have warmed up nicely," Aunt Grace said.

"You shouldn't get in fights," Esther said. "As Christians, we are to live in peace with all men."

"Oh, don't be silly, Esther. Boys will scrap. It gets them ready for war and all. Where would we be if our men didn't know how to fight?"

Esther stared at Aunt Grace. She had thought she would be upset!

"You all just missed the syrup boiling," Aunt Grace said. "Next year you boys will be busy bringing the pails in, and Esther and Ruth and I will be very busy boiling it down."

"You have to boil it down?" Roger asked.

"Oh, yes, it is much too thin to eat right out of the tree.

We will have to boil it down forty to one. Robert, could you explain to Roger what that means?"

Robert's mouth dropped open, but after a few seconds, he began to explain. "That means we will have to bring Esther forty pails of sap from the tree for her to make one pail of syrup."

"Mind you, one pail is a lot of syrup," Aunt Grace added.

"Esther will keep the sap boiling for a long time as most of the sap boils away, and then in the end, she will have syrup."

"Which will make the house smell very nice," Aunt Grace added.

Esther listened to Robert and Aunt Grace discuss the process of making syrup as she searched for a book to read. She couldn't believe that Aunt Grace wasn't upset about the fight, and hadn't asked who Robert had fought with, who had started it, and all that. She had been sure he would get a licking.

Wise people learn when they can; fools learn when they must.
— Duke of Wellington

Chapter Six

THE SCHOOLROOM

"Hurry up with your chores, children, you have school this morning."

Roger looked up from the stall he was 'mucking out,' and then down at his clothes. "Yes, Roger, you will be changing your clothes; now hurry up."

Roger quickly finished that stall and then ran up to change, arriving downstairs before his siblings. "Very good," Aunt Grace said, looking him up and down. Esther and Robert arrived seconds later, and Aunt Grace looked at both of them. "Very good indeed. Now, you know where the school is, just down the street from the church. I told the teacher you would be in today..."

Just then, Ruth came toddling in and went over to Esther, whining. Esther picked her up. "She's rather fussy," Esther said. "Perhaps I should stay home today."

"Nonsense," Aunt Grace said, coming over and taking Ruth. "She will need to learn to stay home with me. Now, off with you all. You don't need to run, but don't dawdle."

Roger raced out of the house and down the road, then

raced back to his brother and sister. "I could have stayed home with her," Esther said. "She's lost mother, and now..."

Roger spun and raced back away, then stopped to look at this really big tree by a bridge. Silly Esther. Ruth would be fine. Maybe she just wanted to get out of school. Which was silly; if she stayed home, she would just have to work all day with Aunt Grace...

"Hey, Roger!" he heard and looked up the road to see Carl racing up the street to him.

"Hey, Carl," he said, charging over to him.

"I hoped you would come today," Carl said. "What's with your sister?"

"Oh, Ruth was fussy, so she thought she should stay home from school with her."

"So she's crying? Oh, I guess since..." Carl trailed off. "What grade are you in?"

"Dunno here, it's our first day. I can read, though."

"Oh, so can I, father would be ever so disappointed if I didn't learn. And mother, oh, she would fuss so. So I can read. I'm not so good at my sums, though."

"I like math. I like reading, too."

"Race you to school," Carl said, and the two took off.

They raced past the church, and Roger saw the school, as well as a teacher. At least he didn't see how she couldn't be a teacher. She was standing in front of a building, wearing a long skirt and a sweater. The yard looked like a schoolyard, with a big bell and all over dirt and stuff marked on the ground.

"And who is this, Carl?" the teacher asked as the boys came racing up and had to stop their race 'cause she was talking to them. She had a big smile on her face, and Roger remembered her from church. She had sat several pews in front of them.

"This is the new Bobtail, Roger," Carl said.

"Very well. I have set up three new desks; you can put him in the one next to you."

Carl raced in, and Roger followed him. Carl went over to a desk on the far right of the room, toward the front. "I guess this is us," he said, looking in the desk. "This is my stuff. That will be you," he said, pointing to the desk next to his.

"Great," Roger said, sitting down, opening the desk, which was empty, then closing the desk and getting up again.

Mommy-Mommy wasn't there. Ruth couldn't find her. Mommy-Esther was gone to school; Ruth had watched her go. But Mommy-Aunt-Grace was here and picked her up and took her everywhere in New Home. And said that Ruth was helping. And gave her plenty to eat.

Esther felt incredibly shy as she walked into the schoolroom with the teacher. There were at least twenty children in the room, with a few older girls, but most of them were Robert's age or younger. And pretty much all of them were looking at her, including her brother Roger, who was sitting next to Carl.

And the room! One room, wooden walls, shelves and hooks all over the place...

"This will be your desk, dear," the teacher said, having walked her almost all of the way to the front of the room and pointing to a desk next to another girl. " I've put you next to Macie. She's a bit younger than you but very friendly. I will give you your books later after I've examined you, but, in the meantime, I put one of our reading books in there so you will have something to do."

Esther sat down, and as she did, she saw that the girl was that girl she had seen running to church, the one with the poor dress and bare feet. And... and she was wearing the same dress, and her feet were still bare. But she had a big smile for Esther, so Esther, hoping her face did not show anything, smiled back.

"Robert," she heard the teacher say before she got a chance to greet the girl, "you will be behind your sister, next to Geoffrey. I believe you are the same age."

Esther and Macie turned to look at the boys, and Esther saw Robert flush. And when he sat down she could see that Geoffrey, who was already seated, looked annoyed.

Geoffrey was very well dressed for school. He had on some kind of suit, way fancier than anyone else was wearing...

"Stand up for the Lord's Prayer, children," the teacher said, and the two girls, along with the rest of the children, stood up.

"Geoffrey?" the teacher said and, to Esther's surprise, it was Geoffrey who started the "Our Father, who art in heaven..." the whole class, including the teacher, saying it with him.

"I suppose now that we have another young man your age, we can have Robert lead us sometimes," the teacher said, and Esther imagined how Robert must be blushing.

When the opening exercises were done, Esther sat down and found the book that the teacher had put in her desk.

"Robert," the teacher said, "I will examine you first. Please come to the front."

Esther looked up from her book as Robert went forward from his new desk but, at a glance from the teacher, looked back down.

"Let me see how you do in this book, Robert," the teacher said. "It is called 'The Jungle Book'[1]. Stand here before me and read."

There were a few seconds of silence and the rustling of pages, and then she heard,

---

Now Rann the Kite brings home the night
That Mang the Bat sets free--
The herds are shut in byre and hut
For loosed till dawn are we.
This is the hour of pride and power,
Talon and tusk and claw.
Oh, hear the call!--Good hunting all
That keep the Jungle Law!
Night-Song in the Jungle

And Robert began the story of the Jungle Book. Esther listened with her book open and noticed that Geoffrey, too, was listening. The longer Robert read, the more angry Geoffrey seemed to get, and finally, she couldn't bear to watch him any more and returned to her book but kept listening and was disappointed when the teacher finally stopped him. "Very good, you will read with the third group. Now say your eight times tables..."

Esther was soon immersed in her book and was rather surprised to hear, some minutes later, the teacher calling Roger up.

She gave him an easier book, a book of children's poetry, which he read in his wild way... very loudly, very quickly, and often putting in the wrong words.

"Very good, you will read in the second group. Now, what is 12 times 10?"

"22!" said Roger.

"Listen more carefully, Roger. I asked what is 12 *times* 10."

"Oh. One hundred and twelve. I mean one hundred and twenty."

"The third time is a charm, it seems. You must take more time to answer, Roger. It does no good to get the wrong answer quickly. Now go to the board and copy the first words of the Declaration of Independence. You see it on that wall, there."

Esther went back to her book but glanced from time to time at Roger's writing. The teacher had gotten busy and then finally looked up at the board.

"Oh, my, Roger, what is that?"

"The declaration," Roger declared, his hands on his hips.

"I suppose it is, after a fashion," the teacher admitted. "But we will have to work on your handwriting. It is dreadful."

"Now let us try your spelling. How do you spell 'train'?"

Roger stood, as Esther knew he would, with his head cocked and an expression on his face as if he was trying to pull something from the depths of his brain.

"T... R... A..." there was a pause "I... N!"

"Yes. Now try 'Develop'."

"D... E... V..." a longer pause "L... no, E again... L... O... P!"

"Very well, you may be seated. You will do your spelling with Macey. Esther?"

Esther came forward, and the teacher asked her to copy the first part of the declaration on the board. She stuck a bit of her tongue out and started, looking back and forth from the wall to the board and writing very carefully. She snuck an occasional glance at the other scholars. Most of them were dressed about the same as she and her brothers were, but about five boys, plus Macey, weren't dressed at all well. They had bare feet, and the boys' clothes were patched where they weren't ripped.

"Very good," the teacher said, startling her. "Now a few math questions. What is seven times eight?"

"Fifty-six," Esther said after a moment's thought. Eights and sevens were hard.

"And twelve times twelve?"

"One hundred forty-four," she said.

"Very good. How do you spell 'dictionary'?"

"D... I... C... T... I... O... N... A... R... Y."

"Excellent. Now let us test your reading."

She handed her the same book Robert had read from. "Start in the middle, please," she said.

Esther leafed through till she came to a page with a picture of a bear and started reading, very slowly and carefully, for she hated to make a mistake,

"Bagheera would lie out on a branch and call, 'Come along, Little Brother,' and at first Mowgli would cling like the sloth, but afterward he would fling himself through the branches almost as boldly as the grey ape."

"Very good, Esther. You will read in the second group with your brother Roger."

Esther went to her seat, flushed with embarrassment. How could she be reading in the same group as Roger?

"Third group," Teacher called, and Robert went forward, as did Geoffrey and four older girls.

"Robert, we are reading from a book called 'Sherlock Holmes,' Have you read it?"

Robert grinned. He had always wanted to read a Sherlock Holmes, but their library at home hadn't carried one. "No, ma'am, but I've heard of it."

"Very well. You are the newest to the group, so you will read first."

Robert noticed that Geoffrey had stood next to him, a scowl on his face, and then the four girls. Teacher handed him a book. "We only have one copy and are starting the third story."

Robert took the book and turned in it to the third story. After a quick glance at the teacher to make sure she was ready for him to read, he started:

A CASE OF IDENTITY[2]

"My dear fellow," said Sherlock Holmes as we sat on either side of the fire in his lodgings at Baker Street, "life is infinitely stranger than anything which the mind of man could invent. We would not dare to conceive the things which are really mere commonplaces of existence. If we could fly out of that window hand in hand, hover over this great city, gently remove the roofs, and peep in at the queer things which are going on, the strange coincidences, the plannings, the cross-purposes, the wonderful chains of events, working through generations, and leading to the most ...

"Let me see," the teacher said when he paused. "Ah, yes, that is a word in French. I believe it is pronounced 'ootray'.

"Thank you," Robert said, "umm, *outré* results, it would make all fiction with its conventionalities and foreseen conclusions most stale and unprofitable."

"Very good. Missy, I know you have been studying some French. Can you tell us what '*outré*' means?"

"It means, like, outrageous or, ummm, bizarre."

"Very well. Now, Geoffrey, what is Mr Holmes trying to say here?"

"Well, fiction is like, books and things that tell stories that aren't true. So he is saying that if we were to look into everyone's houses, we would find stories that would be even stranger than those that someone puts into a book."

"Excellent. Now, Robert, pass him the book."

"And yet I am not convinced of it," I answered. "The cases which come to light in the papers are, as a rule, bald enough, and vulgar enough. We have in our police reports realism pushed to its extreme limits, and yet the result is, it must be confessed, neither fascinating nor artistic."

"A certain selection and discretion must be used in producing a realistic effect," remarked Holmes. "This is wanting in the police report, where more stress is laid, perhaps, upon the platitudes of the magistrate than upon the details, which to an observer contain the vital essence of the whole matter. Depend upon it, there is nothing so unnatural as the commonplace."

"Very good, Geoffrey. Now, Robert, do you recognise the paradox in this paragraph?"

"Umm, there at the end. The words unnatural and commonplace... they mean opposite things but..."

Geoffrey was at the board finishing up some handwriting when recess was called, but everyone else trooped out.

"What's that?" Robert asked George, a younger boy who read with Esther, pointing at a path from the schoolhouse.

"Swimming hole," George replied. "When it gets hot

enough, Teacher lets us boys go swimming. Sometimes the girls get to go instead."

Robert looked around. Roger and Carl had already raced over to a low stone wall and were walking along the top of it, their arms waving wildly. It was bizarre being one of the oldest boys in the whole school. There was just he and Geoffrey...

"I suppose you think you are hot stuff," Robert heard, and he and George turned to see Geoffrey advancing on him.

"What?"

"Being in the third group already," Geoffrey said.

"Reading group?" Robert asked.

"Yes, reading, Dinkus," Geoffrey said.

"It's just a reading group," Robert said.

Geoffrey rolled his eyes dramatically, "Just a reading group. Just the top reading group. Just the reading group which you don't belong in, Bobtail."

"Oh, Geoffrey, you just got in it yourself," Julie said, from where she was standing talking to Esther.

"This is boy talk, Julie!" he said, whirling on her.

Julie rolled her eyes but took Esther by the hand and walked away. Robert set his feet, as it seemed pretty clear that they were about to fight. But, to his surprise, Geoffrey just glared at him for a few seconds and then turned away to the other boys, who had gathered round. "Well?" he asked the boys, "What are we going to play?"

"Dare Base!" Carl shouted, and several others having yelled in agreement, the boys ran around to various trees and things.

"What's Dare Base?" Robert yelled, racing after George.

"Touch the base, and I'll tell you," George yelled, reaching out and putting his hand on the trunk of an old oak tree.

Robert put his hand next to George's, and looked expectantly at him. "It's simple, but fun," he said. "You try to tag people. But you have to have touched your base after they touched theirs. If you get them, then they come to your base."

Robert thought that over for a few seconds as he watched some other boys running around chasing each other. Indeed some of the girls had come over and touched bases, too.

"But why does anyone even leave their base?" he asked.

"Hang on, he's going for a dare," George shouted, and raced after Henry, a small boy who had been coming over near their base. But as he did, Carl jumped away from his own base, the pile of logs sitting ready for the school to burn in their stove, and touched him. George waved ruefully at Robert, went over to the log pile, placed his hand on it, and began looking around eagerly.

"Well, hang it all, how am I going to learn how to..." he saw Henry, who was now fleeing Geoffrey, come racing near and, hoping he understood the rules, raced out and touched him.

"Argh!" Henry yelled as Robert raced back to his own base.

"You don't have to run back, you know," Henry said as he came up to the oak tree. "You get a safe-in coming back after a tag."

"I don't know!" Robert said. "I don't know anything! I've never heard of this game."

Henry chuckled and finished explaining the game.

SOME DOCUMENTS FROM THE CHAPTER
found on next pages

IN CONGRESS, July 4, 1776

The unanimous Declaration of the thirteen united States of America,

When in the Course of human events, it becomes necessary for one people to dissolve the political bands which have connected them with another, and to assume among the powers of the earth, the separate and equal station to which the Laws of Nature and of Nature's God entitle them, a decent respect to the opinions of mankind requires that they should declare the causes which impel them to the separation.

We hold these truths to be self-evident, that all men are created equal, that they are endowed by their Creator with certain unalienable Rights, that among these are Life, Liberty and the pursuit of Happiness.--That to secure these rights, Governments are instituted among Men, deriving their just powers from the consent of the governed, --That whenever any Form of Government becomes destructive of these ends, it is the Right of the People to alter or to abolish it, and to institute new Government, laying its foundation on such principles and organizing its powers in such form, as to them shall seem most likely to effect their Safety and Happiness. Prudence, indeed, will dictate that Governments long established should not be changed for light and transient causes; and accordingly all experience hath shewn, that mankind are more disposed to suffer, while evils are sufferable, than to right themselves by abolishing the forms to which they are accustomed. But when a long train of abuses and usurpations, pursuing invariably the same Object evinces a design to reduce them under absolute Despotism, it is their right, it is their duty, to throw off such Government, and to provide new Guards for their future security.

The Lord's Prayer

Our Father who art in heaven,
hallowed be thy name.
Thy kingdom come.
Thy will be done
on earth as it is in heaven.
Give us this day our daily bread,
and forgive us our trespasses,
as we forgive those who trespass against us,
and lead us not into temptation,
but deliver us from evil.
For thine is the kingdom and the power, and the
*   glory,*
forever and ever.
Amen.

Some people regard private enterprise as a predatory tiger to be shot. Others look on it as a cow they can milk. Not enough people see it as a healthy horse, pulling a sturdy wagon.

— ***Winston Churchill***

Chapter Seven

WORK

"Esther, settle down!"

Esther flushed and did her best to try to concentrate on her spelling. The end of school was taking sooo long! And she knew these words already...

"Very well, it is one o'clock. I will see you all tomorrow."

Esther got up from her desk, put her spelling book in her desk, did her best to walk to the door... and turned and flew down the road, her legs churning out the street.

"Are you home, then?" Aunt Grace asked as she burst into the kitchen. "Watch you don't slam the door."

"Where's Ruth?" Esther gasped, looking frantically around.

"She's napping," Aunt Grace said. "She was looking tired, so I fed her and put her down. You may look..." she said, as Esther started toward the stairs, "... but don't wake her, and come back here and help me get dinner on the table."

"Yes, Aunt Grace," Esther said and dashed upstairs. Sure enough, she peeked in the door, and there was Ruth, sleeping quietly in her cot, her fingers in her mouth.

Esther went back downstairs feeling disappointed, which

was most naughty of her. It was good that she had had a good time... had she?

"How did Ruth do this morning?" she asked Aunt Grace when she entered the kitchen.

"She missed you, naturally," Aunt Grace said. "But I distracted her with making clotted cream, which she found very fun to watch. Then I introduced her to our outhouse... take that plate of corn, please; I opened a can to celebrate your first day at school... where she did very well, if a bit slowly."

"Then we came back inside and did some cleaning of the cool room. I sat her on the cream counter and washed everything. It is very important to keep cheese-making areas clean."

"Then we went outside and walked the fences, which I think she enjoyed. And then, as I said, she got tired, so I fed her her dinner and read her a book while she went to sleep. Which she did quite nicely."

"That's good," Esther said, and Aunt Grace shocked her by giving her a hug.

"You have been doing an excellent job with your little sister, Esther. I am very proud of you."

Esther cried and hugged her back, stopping quickly when she heard the boys in the yard arguing about some game.

"How was your day at school?"

"Oh, umm, fine. Robert got in the first, well, they call it the 'third' reading group."

"Oh, my. On his first day? I hope he is ready for the responsibility."

"What do you mean?"

"The third reading group has a program they put on every year. All the scholars participate, but the third reading group is responsible for it. It is held in the church right before graduation. All sorts of readings... poems, essays, stories scholars have written and published ones. He'll be very busy in a month or so."

Esther flushed. And she had been upset at being excluded!

Suddenly Esther realised that the boys hadn't come in. "What are the boys doing?"

"I told Robert that when they got home, they should go straight to the barn and do some chores while you and I got dinner on. Then we would call them. Go downstairs and get the milk and cream, please."

Esther hurried downstairs, carefully carried a pitcher of milk up, and put it on the table in the dining room. "What are we having?" she asked, carefully lifting the lid of the dutch oven.

"My husband called it 'pâtes au fromage', but in English, we call it 'macaroni and cheese.' But I use a variety of French cheeses and a French sauce, so I think it will taste a bit different than you are used to. Now, run get the cream."

Esther darted off downstairs again and saw Aunt Grace go out the back door as she got back to the kitchen. She went into the dining room, put the cream down at the table, and sat down herself. She almost got up to go get Ruth, but then she remembered that Aunty had fed her already, so she sat back down.

"... And you run all over the place chasing people," Roger was saying as he came in the back door. "Only you should only chase people that left the base before you did. And then, if you catch them, they come to your base. Robert did really well; his base won!"

"On his first day. Well, that's very good. I enjoyed playing Dare Base when I was a girl."

"You played?" Roger asked, his eyes wide.

"I was a girl once, Roger. Perhaps I sat at your desk."

That shut Roger up, and Robert prayed. Esther waited carefully for Aunt Grace to be served and then held out her bowl. She watched, amazed, as Aunt Grace put cream on her mac and cheese!

"Roger, you will need to do Esther's job this afternoon, as she will be beginning to learn how to make cheese with me."

Roger paused in mid-bite to stare at Aunt Grace and then at Esther. "She's going to make cheese?" he asked.

"She's going to start learning," Aunt Grace said. "It is a long hard process to learn all of the various types. It took me a long time to learn it."

"How'd ya learn it?" Roger asked.

"My husband's mother emigrated from France," Aunt Grace said. "From a cheese-making family. She knew all about making cheese, and she taught my husband, and she taught me, once I married into the family. And I will teach Esther and you, Roger."

"Me?" Roger asked, his mouth indecently open and full of food.

"After I get started with Esther. Robert will start with the job of deliveries so he won't learn at first. I'm sure we will get around to teaching him eventually, but you and Esther will have to learn first. Esther will learn first, though, so you will have the watering job today."

"Cool," Roger said. "I like watering the animals."

"How would you know?" Esther asked. "You haven't done it."

"You just think they're all dirty," Roger said. "You're all the time complaining about it."

Esther flushed and looked at Aunt Grace. "Everyone has jobs they like and jobs they don't like. Complaining isn't at all proper or helpful. But neither," she said, looking severely at Roger, "is tattling. Robert, you make sure that Roger finishes his job. You will have both cows to milk, but I will come out later to help finish them off. The cows get impatient if the milking takes too long, especially Giselle. And if we don't finish them off well, they will start giving less milk."

"Yes, ma'am," said Robert, frowning. He wasn't learning milking very quickly!

"Now, Robert, don't be discouraged. Milking is not something that can be learned in a day. Just do your best, and you will find it easy in no time. Or at least before Christmas."

Robert looked up, startled. Had Aunt Grace made a joke? "Yes, ma'am," he said.

"Very good. Now, Esther, come with me."

Esther followed Aunt Grace down the stairs to the cool room. "We will start with a very easy cheese to make," Aunt Grace said. "My mother called it 'Fromage Blanc,' but around here, people call it 'soft-herb cheese.' It doesn't matter what you call it; what matters is how it is made and how it tastes. We start by taking some milk and cream upstairs. I normally make a batch with gallons, but today we will make less than that to practice. And I put an extra cup of cream in with a gallon, so we will need a half cup to go with..."[1]

Twenty minutes later, Esther climbed up on the counter to look at the pot with the 'cheese' in it. It didn't look anything like...

"Come here," Esther, Aunt Grace said. "This is a batch I started yesterday, so you can see how we finish it."

Esther went over to see another identical pot, but what was inside looked very different. "What's that?" She asked.

"That is the whey," her aunt said. "Now we take a pot, set a colander in the top of it, and drape a fine cheesecloth over the colander. Now take this spoon and start getting the curd out of this pot, and put it carefully onto the cheesecloth. While you do that, I will go help poor Robert with the milking."

Aunt Grace walked loudly out of the room and Esther began using the slotted spoon to move the white 'curds' from one pot to the other, where they immediately began draining liquid through the cloth. These curds were interesting, kind of rubbery... she glanced toward the door and took a quick bite... she had washed her hands really well when they started. Not very interesting. Rather bland.

She kept moving the curds and was searching for the last few when Aunt Grace came briskly back in. "Very good," she said, taking the spoon from Esther and quickly getting out the last few bits. "Did you try some?"

Esther blushed and nodded. "Good. It didn't taste bitter or spoiled?" she asked, taking a bite herself.

"No."

"Good. We always check for that. It will taste much better later, after it has drained. We will have some with dinner. I'm sure the boys will enjoy eating the cheese you made. We will put it on the baked potatoes."

Esther stared at the cheese again, "What kind did you say this was?"

"Fromage Blanc, or soft herb cheese."

"How does a cheese get to be hard?"

"Time, dear. Time and pressing. The more you press a cheese, the more liquid you get out of it, so the harder it gets. But the really hard cheeses we age."

Esther nodded and stared some more.

"Now, dear, I want you to go up and get Ruth from her nap. If she sleeps too long, she will not be happy when she tries to go down tonight."

"Yes, Aunt Grace," Esther said, and darted off.

———

"Robert, get yourself and Roger ready for a trip to town."

"Yes, ma'am," Robert said, and left to find Roger.

"Shoes on, Roger, we're going to town," Robert said.

"We are? Where to?"

"I don't know; Aunty didn't tell me. Now..." But Roger was already halfway up the stairs, so Robert went to get his own boots, which were by the front door. He didn't figure he would need his coat for a trip to town in the afternoon. It didn't get cool till later, and he was getting used to it anyway.

He made it out back and saw Roger was already up on the buggy next to Aunt Grace, had the reins and was waiting impatiently for Robert. Robert ran over and jumped up, and Roger said, "Gee up!" Quite loudly, and the horses started.

"Robert, I am going to do my cheese deliveries, which you will be starting to do soon. However, you and Roger need clothes. I have asked our seamstress to be ready for you. Here are ten dollars, which you are to give to her. Then both of you follow all of her instructions.

"Yes, ma'am," Robert said.

But when they got to the seamstress, and she had given them but the quickest glance, she handed Robert two of the dollars and a note. "Take this to the store and bring back what they give you, please."

Robert hurried out and brought the note and the money to the storekeeper. He arrived back to see Roger with a new pair of... he grinned at Robert as the seamstress put another pin in the side of the... "She cut them out while I waited," Roger said. "Just swoop swoop with the scissors..."

"Hold still!" The seamstress said, swatting him as his 'swoop, swoop' motion caused her to miss her next pin.

"Swoop, swoop with the scissors and then started pinning them on me. It was really awesome, two pieces that looked kind of like pants... ouch!"

"Sorry," the seamstress said, "but you really do need to stop moving. I'm almost done."

Robert watched as the seamstress put in two more pins. "There, take those off and I will sew them up tomorrow. Now, you, come over here."

Robert came over and was duly measured as Roger changed. He looked down, surprised, as she measured his feet. "Do you make shoes, too?" he asked.

"No, no. Your aunt asked me to measure your feet and the storekeeper will send away for boots. She says your uncle got you enough underwear?"

Robert reddened a bit, "Yes, ma'am."

"That's good. I do make those too, but you can also buy them from the store. But right now she thinks that you all need work clothes and one set of good clothes for church."

"Yes, ma'am."

"Ruth, you can go back inside and watch Esther," Daddy-Robert said.

Ruth looked for the door and went up to it and went out. Then she looked across the yard. She knew where 'inside' was, Mommy-Aunt-Grace always used the word for going in that door over there. Ruth would go and find Mommy-Esther.

She reached up and opened the door, proud of herself, and went in. Mommy-Esther was there, crying. Why crying?

Ruth smelled a funny smell as she went across and clung to Mommy-Esther's skirts. "Why cry?" she asked, her own tears coming.

"Oh, I'm just... I just burnt something," Mommy-Esther said, drying her eyes with her skirt. "I'm not good at this yet."

"You good," Ruth said, clinging more tightly. Mommy-Esther was good at everything!

"Well, thank you," Mommy-Esther said, her voice happy again. "Let's get this pot washed out."

She picked Ruth up and put her at the sink and Ruth watched Mommy-Esther wash the yucky black out of the bottom of the pot. Mommy-Esther was happy again. That was good.

"Robert, come in here."

Robert looked up from the book he was reading, startled. He always took a few seconds to come back from a book.

He put the book down carefully and hurried into the kitchen, where Aunt Grace was standing at the table with a whole series of packages and papers laid out.

"I need to teach you how we organise our cheese deliveries. You will need to not only know how to deliver this, but also how to label it yourself. I have an order book..."

Ten minutes, ten long minutes, later, Aunt Grace stomped out of the room with a load of cheese, and Robert followed her with his own load, his heart pounding. He couldn't believe he was going to get to do this... or have to do this.... He couldn't decide which it was, whether he was excited or scared to death.

He got his load to the buggy and saw that his Aunt was already sitting on the bench, on the passenger side. Gulping he put his load down and climbed up.

"We'll be going to Mr Thacker first," she said, "Turn right at the end of our driveway, he's at the next farm over."

"Yes, ma'am. Gee up!" Robert said. He didn't say it nearly

as loudly as Roger, but it must have been enough because the horses started down the road.

It was easy enough to get there, he just turned left and then left again at the next driveway, with Aunt Grace saying nothing. In fact, he glanced over, she had taken out a book and started reading it! She wasn't even watching where he was going!

"Well, and who are you?" Robert heard, suddenly, as he was almost to the house. He saw an older man coming out of a long, low barn... one that had openings with several horses sticking their heads out.

He waited a beat for his aunt to answer but, stupid, this man knew who his aunt was! He was asking Robert who he was. And his aunt would expect him to answer for himself. "I'm Robert," he said. "I, umm, I'm starting to learn to do cheese deliveries."

"Well, pull up to the house and let's see what you have for me."

Robert brought the buggy up to the house and jumped out. His aunt just kept reading, obviously trying to get him to learn on his own. He ran to the back of the buggy and searched frantically for the tags that read 'Thacker' as the man stood there, his arms crossed.

He had checked every package twice before he picked up the two that said 'Thacker' and turned to the man. "I'll show you were to put them," he said. "In case you make a delivery when we're not here."

Robert followed the man to the house, expecting at any moment to have some woman come out and greet him, but the man pushed into the screen door alone. "That's our cool box there," he said, pointing to a box in a corner. "Bottom door on the right," he said. "Ice man comes once a week, but that's enough for my needs."

Robert caught the 'my' and took a quick look around the

kitchen and it certainly didn't look like there was a woman that managed this kitchen. It wasn't precisely dirty but it wasn't really clean either.

"Have time for a tour?" Mr Thacker asked, after Robert had put the cheese on the shelf.

"Umm, I don't think so," Robert said. "We have several other deliveries to make."

"Maybe next time then," Mr Thacker said, clapping Robert on the shoulder, then he turned and went back to the barn.

Robert hopped back in the buggy, sure that Aunt Grace would ask him something, but she merely said, "The next deliveries are all town direction," and went back to her book.

"We own the land along this creek," she said, lifting her head and pointing. "We primarily use it for syrup but the wood is also very useful, and we get most of our ice from here."

"Syrup?" Robert asked, staring at the trees.

"Our maple syrup. You will have to learn that job. Up to now Mr Thacker's youngest son has handled it for us. But we certainly could use the income... and the syrup."

Robert's head whirled. He was going to be in charge of gathering the syrup too? So many jobs? Or 'responsibilities' as his aunt was fond of saying.

Aunt Grace seemed busy with some note taking or something, so Robert, who was getting comfortable with driving the buggy down this straight road, spent his time looking around. The road right here was beautiful. The creek ran next to it and a line of tall willows lined the area between the creek and the road, their branches forming a bright green curtain... with some of them hanging in the road itself.

The houses seemed to be all the same fashion as his aunt's; made of wood with heavy beams in the corners. He was used to seeing a lot of brick, but nothing seemed made of brick here.

"Turn in here," his aunt said, startling him, and he turned into a driveway. He had hardly turned before a girl, younger than Esther, was out of the house and racing toward them. He recognised her from school, it was the poor girl who sat by Esther.

"Hello, Mrs Livingston," the girl said, staring at Robert and holding out her hands.

"This is the Gaspine residence," Aunt Grace said, and Robert hopped off the buggy and hurried to the back, finding a small crock with the tag 'Gaspine' on it. He turned around and the girl was there, holding out her hands. He gave it to her but as she turned and started off his Aunt Grace called.

"You forgot the old crock, dear."

"Oh, oh," the girl said, "I'll get it," and ran off.

"She always forgets the crock," Aunt Grace said. "She is too eager to come get the new one. I have to remind her every time. Once I forgot and had to go in the house to get it."

Robert grinned as the girl came racing back holding the crock. He took it and put it in the box in the buggy and got back in and turned the buggy around. This was fun.

"You should know that that is one of the families that keep one of our cows."

"Oh, so we will get that cow back when I get better at milking?"

There was a brief pause. "I think not that one. Indeed I am thinking, with your permission, it would be better to use some of our capital to buy another cow instead."

His permission? She was taking this 'man of the family' thing very seriously. "Ummm, why?" he asked.

"Well, I think it would be an act of Christian charity. That family is rather poor. The father is a hard worker but has some problem with his back and so can't work hard, if you understand what I mean. So having the cow has been very helpful to them. Indeed when I gave it to them I agreed to give them some cheese as well."

"Oh, oh, well that's fine then. And we still get milk from that cow, don't we?"

"Indeed we do."

"Well, that's fine then. Maybe we could have Esther deliver the cheese here sometimes, she and that girl sit together at school."

"Ah, yes, that would be good."

Three hours later, he was driving back to their house with a light heart. He had delivered all of the cheese and, with Aunt Grace watching carefully, had added three orders to their order book.

"Stop at the seamstress," Aunt Grace said suddenly, as he got into town. "She sent me a note; she wants to take some more measurements."

"Yes, ma'am," Robert said, looking around and finally remembering where it was. He pulled the buggy up beside the house and jumped down, Aunt Grace following him. He tied the reins to the bar in front of the house and followed Aunt Grace into the house.

As the seamstress pulled and pinched at Robert's new pants and discussed various sewing things with Aunt Grace, Robert looked in the mirror, which stood right in front of the box she had him stand on, and looked at the clothes she had already made. The one he had on was a church outfit, but not like what he would have worn back home. It was, like, super sturdy cloth. He didn't know the names of any of this stuff, but this stuff felt like it would last forever. He supposed that she was hoping he could pass it down to Roger.

For the briefest of instants, his eyes thought about crying, but he stuffed the tears down. The idea of them still living here when Roger was big enough for this suit reminded him that his parents were dead.

"OK, next," Aunt Grace said, with her sharp tone, and Robert hurriedly put on the next outfit, which was a work outfit. This lady had made him half a dozen sets! He supposed that made some sort of sense; the clothes that Uncle Robert had bought were much more flimsy, more made for town. "Oh, and Robert, try on the boots with that set."

Robert sat down and pulled on the boots. Nice, high boots. Good for the farm. No chance that too much muck would get in. He hated it when that happened. But more, he hated it that he was really starting to like it. That was stupid, but it was how he felt. He had really enjoyed delivering cheese, which somehow made him feel like a traitor to his parents.

"Turn around," the seamstress said, finding even more places for her pins.

"Only the dead have seen the end of war."
— Plato

Chapter Eight

THE STORM

R oger woke up... slowly. Which he never did. He always bounced right out of bed. He tried to sit up, but his head swam, and his stomach did a backflip, so he lay back.

"Robert," he moaned. "I'm sick. I need a bucket."

Robert darted out of bed, and Roger heard him in Aunt Grace's room, then heard him pounding off downstairs, coming back a minute later with a bucket.

"Here," Robert panted out, just as Aunt Grace, in her nightgown, came in and looked worriedly down at him, followed by Esther.

"What is wrong with you, Roger?" Aunt Grace asked as Esther pushed past her and felt his forehead.

"My stomach..." Roger moaned.

"And he has a fever," Esther pronounced.

"Well, we don't all need to be here. Robert, Esther, you get dressed and do your chores so you can go to school. Roger, I will bring you... I will make you some lemonade," she declared and stomped off downstairs. It was amazing how she could stomp in her bare feet.

A few minutes later, Roger heard her feet on the stairs and opened one eye to see Aunt Grace with a glass. She looked down at him. "I, well, here is your lemonade. Would you like to sleep in the bed, since you're sick?"

Roger shook his head, and then used the bucket.

"Oh, dear. Would you like a wet towel?"

"Yes..." Roger whispered, not being willing to nod his head again.

"Very well," Aunt Grace said and clumped back out.

Aunt Grace brought him the wet towel and, very awkwardly, patted his forehead with it. "Are you... do you feel worse?"

"Oh, I feel..." Roger started to reach down to clutch his stomach, but Aunt Grace looked so funny... so... worried, that he stopped and said, "I think I just want to sleep for a while."

"Oh, yes, very good; I'm sure that will make you feel better," she said, and stomped out, Roger staring after her. What was up with Aunt Grace?

"Here he is," Roger heard, a long time later, and rolled over to see the preacher's wife! She was carrying her baby, and Roger heard two other children arguing downstairs. What was she doing here?

"Well, let's see what is going on with our young lad here," the preacher's wife said and handed the baby to Aunt Grace, who took it rather reluctantly. "How are you feeling, lad?"

"Awful," Roger moaned. He hated being sick, but he loved acting sick.

"Well, that isn't very helpful," the preacher's wife said, feeling his forehead. "You are hot. Have you thrown up?"

Roger nodded, which his stomach didn't like.

"Have you been drinking? What have you been drinking?"

"Lemonade," Aunt Grace said firmly. "I thought it was better than milk."

Roger thought he saw a funny look on the pastor's wife's

face, but what she said was, "That's true, milk is not recommended. Whey might be OK. Lemonade certainly might be easier to get down. How has he been tolerating it?"

"He hasn't drunk much," Aunt Grace admitted.

"Well, let's try some whey and some water," the preacher's wife said. "We can leave all three here for him to choose between. Sick bodies sometimes know what they need. Have you been passing water?"

Roger nodded.

"Well, let's get some of these blankets off, and I will sit with you. Grace, if you could bring us some water and whey and watch my two little ones, this one wants to nurse."

Aunt Grace stomped off downstairs, and the preacher's wife began to nurse her fat baby.

"Why did you come?" Roger asked her.

"Your aunt told Robert to ask Carl to ask me to come," she replied, adjusting the baby. "Your Aunt has not yet dealt with a sick child, so she wanted me here. I have had my share. Why, my Geoffrey, when he was three years old, was sick unto death for three weeks. And Carl, who is your age, got the scarlet fever just last year."

Roger guessed that it made sense that a lady with all those kids would have seen sick kids. He reached down and sipped the lemonade.

"Do your best to drink, child; it will help you get better faster."

Roger took another few sips and picked up his book. Not Toby Tyler, his aunt said he had to save that one for their all-together times. This one was a silly poetry book called 'Father Goose Poetry'.[1] It *was* very silly.

> *"Did you ever see a rabbit climb a tree? Did you ever see a Lobster ride a flea? Did you ever? No you never. For they couldn't, don't you see."*

Silly.

"Well, you seem to be doing well with the lemonade," he heard about an hour later, and looked up, startled. The preacher's wife had put her baby on the couch and was reaching over to feel his forehead. "I think the fever is breaking," she said. "You look sweaty. I think you just have that fever which is going around. It makes one miserable for about a day, and then you get better rather quickly. I will go and get you something to eat, and we will see how you handle it."

Roger sat up. He did, indeed, feel better. Almost hungry.

And then the preacher's wife came back, followed by an anxious-looking Aunt Grace. "Here, try a spoon full of this," the preacher's wife said, handing him a bowl of applesauce.

He took a spoon, smelled it, tasted it, and then ate it. He was reaching for more when the preacher's wife took it away. "No, no, not yet. We'll give that half an hour."

She turned to Aunt Grace. "I think you can handle this now. Just let him eat one spoonful every half an hour or so if he doesn't vomit. He should keep drinking. By supper time, if he feels like it, he will be ready for a regular meal. The others will probably come down with this next, so you know what to look for. Only light sheets, offer several things to drink; applesauce is a good first meal."

"Umm, yes, yes, very well," Aunt Grace said, watching the preacher's wife leave. "You are doing better? Can I get you anything?" she asked Roger.

"Another book?" he asked, holding up the Father Goose book.

"Very well," she said, and clumped off, Roger watching her and grinning. To think, Aunt Grace was afraid of his getting sick!

"Roger!" Esther said, her voice almost a shriek. "What have you been doing?"

"Butcher!" Roger said, holding up a dead, mostly plucked, very bloody bird. Roger himself was covered with blood and, eww, and feathers. He had a rather large feather sitting on the top of his hair.

"What? Well, go out to the pump and wash the bird. I will come get it, and you can wash."

"OK," Roger said, going back out the door. Esther spent a frantic few seconds washing the floor and then darted out to the pump, followed more slowly by Ruth.

"Where did you get the chicken?" she asked Roger as he rather fruitlessly washed the bird in the pump. She leaned forward and worked the handle for him so he could rub the bird.

"Aunty showed me which one to take," he said. "She said this one hasn't been laying. Dunno how she knew. Had me catch it and cut its head off. Then she showed me how to pluck it... that took a long time! Then how to cut all the guts out. Had me put them in a bucket which she took to the manure dump."

"Oh." Esther was very, very glad that she hadn't had to do that herself. Although, no doubt she would have done a better job of it!

"Why kill chicken?" Ruth asked.

"Gonna eat it, Ruthy!" Roger said, handing Esther the chicken.

Esther put it back under the water, which Roger then pumped, and worked to get the last bits of filth off of the outside the chicken, and then started working on the cavity.

"Maybe chicken pot pie, or maybe chicken and dumplings, or maybe chicken soup..." Roger said.

"Oh!" Ruth said. "I like soup."

"I like all of them," Roger said, which Esther knew Ruth did too, but couldn't really say.

"Aunty said this was going to be one of my jobs!" Roger said proudly. "Said as how you wouldn't probably like it and were too busy with cheese. And Robert would be too busy delivering and doing wood, so that left me. She let me use the knives! Said I had to be really careful, which I was. I didn't even cut myself!"

Esther shuddered. Letting Roger play with sharp knives. Well, that wasn't fair; he wasn't playing—he was working. Maybe this way, they would get to eat more chicken! That would be nice.

───────

Roger sat on Robert's bed, book in hand, looked out the window at the pouring rain, and cried. His mother had always hated rainy days. Roger never could manage to stay quiet, and she would spend a half an hour telling him to and then break down and lick him, sometimes three times in the same afternoon. And here he was being quiet; he even had a book he had been reading, because his mother wasn't here to lick him.

Every time he had even thought about making noise and racing around the house, he had been reminded that his mother wasn't here to yell at him. He stared down the road but, no matter how hard he stared, his mother and father didn't walk down the road, arm in arm, an umbrella between them.

How could she do it? How could his mother have gone away... to heaven, Esther would say... but how could she have gone away at all? He had been playing at the neighbours, and then Uncle Robert had come and taken them away, and everyone had told him that she was dead. She and father, but father was just father; how could mother be gone?

He heard loud clumping steps and quickly wiped his face and opened his book.

"Oh, good, Roger, you are here," he heard. "I need a boy that isn't afraid of going out in the rain and climbing the roof, and I thought of you."

He grinned and jumped up. Climb the roof? In the rain! "What roof?"

"The barn roof. There is a leak, and I see the water from it every time it rains, but I can't find it when it isn't raining. So I need you to climb up to the hay loft and find it, and then I will give you some tar to go up on the roof with, and we will see if we can't close the leak.

"Awesome!" he said, racing downstairs for his wellies.

He climbed quickly up into the top loft of the barn, his aunt climbing more slowly behind him, and Robert following both of them. Thunder roared through the windows, although it seemed to be getting farther and farther away. He stood up and spun around, looking for the leak... "There it is!" he shouted, pointing to water running down the wall to his left.

"There the water is," his aunt agreed, "But where is the leak?"

"What do you mean...?" he asked, then ran over to the wall to look at the water. Sure enough, it wasn't coming out of the roof, it was running down a beam. He tried to jump up and look up the beam, but he couldn't see anything, so he took off his wellies, went over, and shinnied up the wall beam, then hooked his hands and legs over the beam where the water was coming down, and started to crawl, upside down, up the beam.

"It's still wet here," he said, three 'steps' later, feeling the beam with his hand.

"Well, keep going then," his aunt said, and Roger kept going.

"Well, it's dry here," he said, when he was almost at the top.

"Go down some and see where it is coming from!" Robert yelled at him, cupping his hands to make his voice heard over the noise of the storm.

"Here it is!" Roger yelled, excited, about a foot below where he had felt last. "I can feel it dripping on my hand."

He pulled his head up, and sure enough, he could even see a bit of light... a flash of lightning... through the roof. "There's a leak here!" he shouted.

"Come down then!" his aunt yelled.

Roger quickly shinnied back down, and his aunt handed him a pot and a stick. A kind of flat stick. "You need to go out on the roof and fill in the crack," she said.

"Now?" he asked.

"It won't do much good to wait. We know where it is now, and we will be able to tell if it stops leaking."

"But he might fall!" Robert said, his eyes wide.

"I won't fall!" Roger scoffed, although not at all convinced he wouldn't.

"We will tie a rope to him," his aunt said. "The leak isn't far from the window."

They all looked at the shutter, which was banging in the wind. "This roof was always leaking, so my husband put walking boards on it, so it shouldn't be difficult for an active boy like you. Here, let me tie this rope to you and Robert, and I will hold it after I loop it around this beam."

Roger watched, wide-eyed, as his aunt tied the rope to him, looped it around the beam, and handed the other end to Robert. Then he followed her to the window, which she opened, causing a torrent of rain to spray in their faces. "There is the ladder, Roger," she shouted, and Roger leaned out of the window and saw the ladder.

Roger gulped. He loved climbing and doing fun and dangerous things, but... a spray of water hit him in the face again and then went down his collar. This was cold!

He turned to suggest to his aunt that, perhaps, he shouldn't... but she was staring at him with such a look that, instead, he gulped again and reached out of the window, grabbing the ladder.

He had taken his wellies off when he had climbed up to the top loft, so it was easy to swing his feet over and grip with his toes. Torrents of water went down the back of his shirt and cascaded all the way down past his ankles. Freezing water!

He climbed one careful rung after another and was about to climb on the roof when he heard his aunt yelling and looked down. She was handing him the pot! That would have been stupid!

He reached down and grabbed the pot and stick and, the stick firmly in the pot where it stuck really well, he put the pot on the roof and climbed after it.

He could see the beams at the top of the roof, and it was the third beam in, so he knew where to go and carefully, very carefully, crawled over and started looking.

He looked up, higher than the board he was on, and a gust of wind blew his jacket and shirt up, sending rain all up his back, but he didn't see anything, so he leaned down and looked below the board. Nothing either. But he knew it was there, and then, suddenly, he saw a crack of light... right at the top of the board he was on!

He took the pot, took the stick out, got a big gallump of the tar stuff, and mushed it down next to the board. Then he put the stick back in the pot, reached his hand down, and pushed it all over.

His hair fell into his eyes, and, without thinking, he reached up to push it back. Oh, wow, now he had tar on his face!

He reached back down and pushed and pushed, mushing it all in all over, and then, hoping that worked, started inching his way back to the window.

He got there and looked over, and Robert was there yelling. "You did it!" he shouted, "give me the pot!"

Roger handed the pot down and slid one foot over. His toes poked into the empty air until he felt a hand grab his foot and move it... ah, there was the rung. He slid his other foot over and got the rung on his first swing. Then he lowered himself...

And slid. But he felt a hand holding him up by his belt loop, and he hung for a second in mid-air and then crashed down, on top of Robert, into the barn.

Robert looked up at him, a bit winded, and then burst into laughter. "Oh! Your face!" he said. "You have tar all over it!!"

"And you are both soaked," his aunt said, her voice sharp and matter-of-fact. "Come inside. I have Esther warming up bath water for you, Roger, and you, Robert, can dry off by the fire."

Roger and Robert had stripped off, and Robert, swathed in towels, had gone off to the parlour as Roger climbed into the tub Esther had filled with hot water.

Roger was just in when the door opened, and his aunt came in, book in hand, "I want you to take a long soak," she said. "So here is a book. I will tell Esther to refill your water when it gets cold.

"What ya cooking?" Roger asked from the tub. Esther was very glad that Aunty had not asked *her* to climb up on the roof and get soaking wet. They would be lucky if Roger didn't catch a cold!

"I haven't decided," she said, opening yet another cupboard to try to help herself decide.

"Dinner?"

"No. Aunty will be cooking dinner. I will be making... something. Aunty said I could decide what."

"To go with dinner?"

"No. She said it could be sweet or savoury, and we would eat it in the parlour after dinner."

"Dessert?"

"Yes..." Esther said.

"Can you make a pie? We have lots of strawberries!"

"Strawberry pie? I never have done."

"Well, that's no reason not to do something," Aunt Grace said, bustling in from the cold room and putting a large pot on a counter. "What is it that you haven't done?"

"Made a strawberry pie. Roger says we have lots of strawberries."

"Very true. We got a very good crop last year, and I put up a lot. They will be producing again in June, so we certainly can use some now. A good choice."

Esther watched her as she clumped down to the cool room—watched her hoping that she would tell her what to do! Mother never did this! Her mother would walk her through everything. Her mother would never have let Roger get up on that roof! Her mother... was dead.

She turned away from Roger to hide her tears and thought frantically. Well, first of all, if it were all that hard, then Aunt Grace would never let her waste good food getting it wrong. So it must not be that hard. And... and she knew how to make pie crusts. They had practiced that enough.

She got out the flour and started working on the pie crust while she thought. She added extra sugar to the crust because this was NOT a savoury dish. It was a dessert and meant to be sweeter, and she didn't think the extra sugar would hurt the crust at all.

She laid the bottom crust in the pan and then went to get the strawberries. At least she knew where they were. In the cool room, in the second room, on the bottom shelf, in the back.

She came back into the kitchen and looked at the jar, then looked at the pie. Yes, this jar would do, she thought. And if not, well, she could go get another jar!

She opened it up and looked at it. It had obviously been canned in the juice, not just water.

"What you got?" Roger asked.

"A jar of strawberries," Esther said, trying to sound as if she knew what she was doing. She tasted the juice...

"Can I have a taste?"

Well, she didn't see why not. He might even make a helpful comment. She took a small spoon and put some juice in, and walked it over to Roger, watching him as he tasted it.

"Nice and sweet," he declared. "Will the strawberries be that sweet, too?"

"No," she said, finally realising it herself. "You add sugar to make the juice come out. I will have to add more sugar to the pie to make it a good sweetness."

She dumped the strawberries in and had a moment's panic, wondering if she should have sliced them. But, no, she was making this; she could make it with whole strawberries if she wanted to.

She got out another half cup of sugar as Aunty didn't like using too much sugar for things, almost the only thing she didn't like them eating, and had just dusted it on when Aunty returned. "Looking good," she said. "You may use the rhubarbs that we put up if you wish. Don't use more than a half cup or so, or it will be too tart."

"I think I want it sweet," Esther said, considering.

"That is fine, dear," Aunty said, and clumped back out.

Esther carefully cut up the top crust and braided it on. By the time she was halfway done, Roger was there, wrapped in his towel and staring. "That looks good!" he said.

"Well, I'm glad you think so. I hope it will taste just as good."

"I'm sure it will," he said, racing off upstairs.

"I don't see why it shouldn't," she said to herself. "It is just strawberries, sugar, and crust. If I didn't make the crust too tough, it should be fine. And since Ruth wasn't helping me, the crust shouldn't be too tough."

She took one last look and slid the pie into the oven, just underneath the dutch oven Aunty had put in earlier. Now she just had to remember to take it out on time...

But how long would it cook? She had a moment's panic and then realised that she knew how long a pot pie took to cook. She would just check it a little before that. Most of what you looked for was the crust, anyway!

She paced around the kitchen, then went into the dining room and set the table, then came back into the kitchen... to see Aunty taking her Dutch oven out of the oven and glancing at her pie.

"How... how is it?" she asked her.

"I will let supper sit for a few minutes, and then it will be ready. You have the table set?"

"Yes, ma'am."

Aunt walked out, leaving Esther very frustrated. She opened the oven and peeked, but naturally, her pie was nowhere near done.

"Esther, bring the Dutch oven out, please," she heard

several minutes later and, frustrated, grabbed a pot holder and took it out.

Everyone else was there, even Ruth, and as soon as she put it down and sat down, Robert prayed, and he and Roger passed things out. Esther moodily took a bite of the potato soup that she hardly tasted.

"Is your pie ready_ yet, Esther?" Roger asked, gulping down a bite before speaking.

"Don't be silly, Roger," Aunty said. "A pie takes about an hour to cook, and then she will need to leave it out for a few minutes before serving so you won't burn your mouth. We will be eating it after our evening reading."

"Oh," Roger said, and, her heart singing, Esther took another spoonful of the soup. It was very good, actually. It had bits of ham, bacon, and chicken in it; along with potatoes, onions... she peered carefully... and cheese. Well, certainly it had cheese in it; pretty much everything they ate did. Cheese, whey, sour cream...

"After dinner, Esther, you can whip up some cream. I have taught you to do that?"

"Oh, yes, ma'am," Esther said.

"It will go very well on it, I think."

Esther waited patiently for everyone to be done eating dinner and then rushed off to the kitchen to make the cream. She gave a quick glance at her pie, but as Aunty had said, it wasn't done. She got out the cream, added some sugar, whipped it up, and took it into the parlour where Aunty and the boys were sitting around reading, with Robert reading to Ruth. Then she went back and looked at her pie again... oh, wonderful, it was bubbling up, and the crust was just turning brown!

She took it out and carefully carried it into the parlour. Aunty took a glance and went back to her reading. Roger started to get up but stopped at a glance from Aunty and went back to his book. Esther hurried back, got out the pie plates and forks and then went to the cool room and got out the lemonade, bringing it all back to the parlour.

"You will need glasses as well," Aunty said, and Esther, blushing, went back to get them.

Then she sat down and nervously tried to read, feeling very happy indeed when Aunty said, some minutes later, "Very well, I think we can eat the pie now. Robert, if you could serve it?"

Esther itched to do it herself, but sat primly still as Robert served Aunty, and Roger got up to give out the lemonade.

"We won't normally be eating in the parlour," Aunty said, taking a bite with no comment, "But this is a special occasion, with Esther cooking her first special dish. Now, children, after you tell her it is very good, you also need to tell her what she might have done differently."

Esther blushed furiously, taking her own bite now that Robert had given it to her. It was, well, it was almost sort of undercooked! But she had... the crust was perfect!

"It's great, Esther," Roger said, "But you could have put in more strawberries."

"Strawberries tend to settle, that's true," Aunty said.

"Ummm, it's great," Robert said. "I don't know... You could have made more of it," he grinned.

"No, she couldn't. One pie is quite enough. Esther?"

"It... it seems a little undercooked?"

"That's true and false," Aunty said. "Some people make it just like this, and it is wonderful. Others cook the strawberries down, or even just some of the strawberries down, first. I'm sure you can imagine what that would do."

"It would be more... more like jam?"

"Exactly. It is up to you to decide how you like it or how your audience would like it. But this was very well done."

Flushing, Esther ate the rest of her piece and even allowed Robert to give her another little one. Her first special dish! And she had done it right!! Her mother... her mother would have been so proud! And her father would have loved to eat it, just like Roger.

Oh, bother, she was crying. And everyone was avoiding looking at her. This was so embarrassing!

Esther sat in their pew, feeling very conscious of her new dress. She had schooled herself not to think of all the things she had lost in the explosion: her dolls, her books, and her clothes. Indeed her one pillow which had been a gift from Aunt Lydia. Her parents had died in that explosion, and it seemed sacrilegious to worry about anything else in that light.

But she had been very aware that she had no real Sunday clothes, just the town dress that Uncle Robert had bought for her. Which was fine in its way but was not a church dress.

So she had been very pleased, and had tried not to show it, when Aunt Grace sent her to the seamstress and ordered both a work and a church dress.

And she felt like everyone was looking at her in it, so she did her best to focus her attention on the visiting preacher who sat with Geoffrey's father at the front of his church. His suit was rather ragged, as were the clothes of the eight children that sat with his wife in the front row. If she understood correctly, only the three smallest children were his, the other five were from the orphanage he ran. She shuddered at the idea that she and her siblings might have had to go to an orphanage, and sleep in big cold bunk rooms with all sorts of crying children and wet beds and the like.

The last hymn sung, the visiting preacher got up, arranged

his notes on the pulpit, looked out at them (she felt like he was looking at her!) and began preaching...

The Orphan's Father[2]

"For in thee the fatherless findeth mercy."-- Hosea xiv. 3.

THE Lord God of Israel, the one only living and true God, has this for a special mark of his character, that in him the fatherless findeth mercy. "A Father of the fatherless, and a Judge of the widows, is God in his holy habitation." False gods of the heathen are usually notable for their supposed power or cunning, or even for their wickedness, falsehood, lustfulness, and cruelty; but our God, who made the heavens, is the Thrice Holy One. He is the holy God, and he is also full of love. Indeed, it is not only his name, and his character, but his very nature, for "God is love." Among the acts which exhibit his love is this-- that he executeth righteousness and judgment for all that are oppressed, and specially takes under his wing the defenceless ones, such as the widow and the fatherless.

... A half an hour later she was very glad when he said...

Now, lastly, here is ENCOURAGEMENT AS TO WHAT TO EXPECT OF GOD. "In thee the fatherless findeth mercy."

What do the fatherless expect of us when we stand in God's place to them, and take them into our Orphanage, and try to be as a father to them? What do they expect of us? Well, I do not know that the younger ones have intellect enough to know all they expect, but they expect everything. They expect all that they want, and though they do not quite know what they do want, they leave it to us. They believe that all will be found that they require. I like a poor Christian who does not know all he wants; but yet knows that his God will supply all his needs. He trusts Jesus for all. He trusts his heavenly Father as a child: he does not know what he may require to-day, and require in the unknown future, but then his heavenly Father knows, and he leaves it all to him. As our orphan boys grow older, however, they begin to have a perception of their wants, and they trust that they shall have everything provided which their own fathers would have provided for them, and more, perhaps. So is it with men when we come to the great Father. We say: all that I would provide for my children, if I had everything, and could give them all that wisdom could desire, my God will provide for me, for he will be a Father to me. If ye, being evil, know how to give good gifts unto your children, much more shall he, who has taken you into his family, though you once were fatherless, give all good things to you. You shall have food and raiment, and sufficient for this life. You shall have protection, guidance, instruction, and tender affection. You shall have a touch or two of the rod every now and then, and that is among your choice mercies; but you shall also have all the cherishing of his sweet love; and by-and-by, when you are fit for it, he will take you home from school, and you shall see his face, and you shall live for ever in his house above, where the many mansions be. Oh, if you come and put yourselves by a simple faith into the blessed custody and keeping of God, he will admit you into his Salvation Orphanage, and he will take care of you, and you shall find him a better Father than you will be to your own children-- a better Father than the best of fathers could ever be to the best beloved of sons. "I will be a Father unto you, and ye shall be my sons and daughters, saith the Lord Almighty." I will not say more, but I should like to leave John's choice sentence as my last word. "Behold what manner of love the Father hath bestowed upon us, that we should be called the sons of God!" Blessed be thy name, O Lord, that we also have been led of thy Spirit to prove that in thee the fatherless findeth mercy!

The sermon finished, Geoffrey's father stood up to lead them in the last hymn, and she felt as if everyone must be looking at them, at her specifically, her face no doubt a flaming red. To have a whole sermon preached about orphans!

Robert wished that he had not had to sit next to Aunt Grace during that sermon, and was quite glad when the visiting preacher read the benediction, and everyone got up from their seats and started walking out. Aunt Grace,  along with a dozen other people, went over to the visiting preacher. Roger, annoyingly, did too, although not to the preacher but to the kids he brought with him, no doubt inviting them to come out and swing or whatever.

Esther, holding Ruth by the hand, was right behind Robert as he wove his way through the crowd and out into the yard. Oh, how he wished there wasn't going to be a potluck today, prolonging his agony. A sermon on orphans! He had never been so embarrassed in his life. It almost made it worse that everyone was oh so carefully avoiding looking at him.

Just then, a cool wind and light rain hit him, so he hurried over to the tables where there was a permanent roof. I guess the church didn't want their meals to get all wet.

"Not everyone can get a whole sermon preached about them," he heard, and turned to see Geoffrey, followed by a dozen children, coming toward him. Or, rather, probably, coming toward the shelter Robert was standing under. But they all heard Geoffrey, and Robert flushed.

"Well, maybe, being a preacher's kid, you should listen to it," he said, and turned away and walked over to the table. But a minute or so later he heard,

"Did you hear me, Bobtail?"

Robert turned toward Geoffrey. "Ummm, no."

Geoffrey flushed, "I said..."

"I don't really care what you said," Robert put in before Geoffrey could repeat whatever nonsense he had been saying, "Does anyone?"

Geoffrey flushed, "Just because you..."

"Robert," Esther said, pushing between the boys, "Could you help me..."

"Hiding behind your sister?" Geoffrey snorted, "Afraid to..."

"What are you talking about? You're the one who runs around in those fancy clothes trying to act all special."

"You're the ones that came to our town even though we didn't want you here. Living with Mrs Livingston. Just because your mother is dead..."

Robert heard a scream, and before he could even turn to look, Roger had head-butted Geoffrey, and the two went tumbling down into a mud puddle. Robert stared in shock as Roger's arms windmilled up and down, pummelling Geoffrey.

"You don't get to talk about my mother!" Roger screamed, and, his shock gone, Robert leapt forward and pulled a struggling Roger off Geoffrey.

"Look what your snot-nosed brother did to my clothes," Geoffrey shouted, leaping up and advancing on the boys. "I'm going to thrash him... Ow!"

Geoffrey struggled frantically, but his father had him painfully by the ear. The entire crowd watched his father drag him off to the north wall of the church.

"You stand here and wait for me to finish my dinner, young man!" his father said, turning him toward the wall and releasing him. "I am going to dinner, and when I'm done eating, you and I will discuss this incident in my office."

Robert stared in shock at Geoffrey, who stood facing the church wall, trembling with anger. Or perhaps embarrassment. And occasionally stomping one foot and moving his head as if he was talking to himself. The pastor had done that? And it was raining, too!

Geoffrey walked stiffly upstairs, tears flowing down his face and furious. His father never licked him! Stupid Bobtails!! They come to town, and suddenly his teacher, his father, and even his stupid siblings were all over him about being nice and polite and making friends.

How could he make any friends! He was a preacher's kid! Everyone always looked at him funny, either asking him questions about the sermon... as if he knew or cared... or shutting all up when they would normally have sworn... as if he cared.

Not that he dared swear, obviously! Not being a preacher's kid. The moment he stepped the least bit out of line, the entire village was talking about it. He couldn't do anything that the other boys did. Why, one stupid old lady had even said to his mother that he shouldn't go swimming! Something about carnal temptations or some such. Luckily his father had heard her and launched into some long sermonette about natural behaviour being a something to avoid something else and how even David had peed against a tree or something like that. He forgot the reference. But anyway, anyone else would have just said, 'boys will be boys' and shut the stupid old lady up, but his father had to give a sermon.

Just like now. Instead of just getting a licking for being rude, he had gotten a half an hour sermon about the golden rule, and pure and undefiled religion meaning being nice to orphans... and then gotten licked! And the worst licking he had gotten in, well, since those stupid orphans had arrived and Mrs Livingston had heard him mouthing off about that little girl. Which had been pretty stupid on his part. He knew as well as any boy that a boy fight was one thing, but you couldn't insult girls or little kids. Or widows. Well, they were girls.

He opened his door and threw himself on his bed before noticing that Carl was there at his desk, drawing or something. He turned toward the wall and did his best to stop crying.

"You caught it good," Carl said.

"Shut it, Carl!"

"I don't know why you are so down on the Bobtails," Carl said. "I'd think you'd like it having a new boy your own age and in your reading group and all. Better than all girls."

"Shut it, Carl!"

"I mean, you two could go fishing and everything. You were always complaining that the bigger boys never wanted to go, they being too busy with work and all."

"Shut it, Carl!"

"And just think, if you got to be friends, you might get to eat over; and you know how well Mrs Livingston cooks."

Not even Geoffrey would defend his mother's cooking. She seemed to think that preacher's kids should be skinny and kept them that way by tasteless cooking and small portions.

"You just like being special and different and all. I don't know why."

Maybe because he had always been special? Oldest of the preacher's kids, always dressed up by his mother like some doll... that was the way the other boys had always talked about it, anyway. So he'd figured he might as well learn to like it, he couldn't fight against it. And he was good at reading! Why did some other kid have to arrive that was his age, good at reading... and an orphan! How could he compete against that? The whole church, the whole stupid village had been talking about the stupid orphans before they even came, how wonderful Mrs Livingston was to take them (no one had called Mrs Livingston wonderful before that. Well, except when she brought food.), how horrible it had been for the orphans, how nice everyone would have to be to them, and to never, ever mention their parents.

Argh.

Carl went back to drawing, and Geoffrey finally got done crying but just lay there. Eventually, he heard a door close downstairs... must have been whomever father was counselling. People were coming all the time, in and out of Father's special door. Men and couples... never women alone, certainly. That would be indecent or some other big word...

"Geoffrey!" he heard, and sat up. Carl was staring at him.

"Father wants you back again?" he said, awe in his voice. "What did you do?"

"Nothing... nothing more, anyway. And he already licked me for that."

"Geoffrey?"

"Coming!" Geoffrey called and quickly wiped his face with his handkerchief and hurried downstairs.

Robert lay in his bed, drawing in his journal. His rather messy bed. He was trying to draw a picture of the barn that didn't come out all lopsided. But somehow, between the ground and the roof, everything managed to get, as Roger would say, 'all cattywampus.'

He looked over at Roger, lying on his back on the couch, his sheets snarled up around him, laying on his back and pretending he was riding a bicycle, his legs pumping furiously. It being Sabbath, with the limited chores they did on that day, no one was particularly tired. Or sleepy. And Robert's mind was still whirling from the big fight they had had at church.

Esther walked into the boys' room, and Robert stared at her. "Esther, are you OK?" Her face was white!

She turned around and closed the door. Which even made Roger look serious.

"What's wrong?" Robert said.

"I don't know if I should tell you," Esther said. "It's like eavesdropping except, you know, it was something I saw."

She wiped her eyes, and Robert realised she had been crying. "What did you see?" Roger asked, getting off his bed and coming over to sit by Robert.

"I... it was Aunt Grace. She was... she was writing this letter, and she was crying. She didn't know I was there, and at first I didn't even know anything was going on, but anyway she didn't see me, and I saw her, and she was writing this letter, and she was crying."

"Why?" Roger asked.

"I don't know why! She never saw me, which, oh, I suppose that was naughty of me; I should have said something or something."

The three of them all sat there wondering. They had

never seen Aunt Grace cry before! Or, rather, the boys hadn't. Esther had seen her a few times... but that was in bed when she was no doubt thinking about their parents and all—not writing a letter!

"Maybe she's mad at us," Roger said. "People cry when they're mad sometimes."

"But what was the letter?" Robert asked.

"Maybe she was apologising for the fight," Roger said, sounding worried. "She never did lick either of us. Maybe she was too mad to lick us."

"She didn't say anything about it," Esther protested.

"Maybe she's mad because I eat too much," Roger said.

"Oh, don't be silly, Roger. She loves it when you eat. She just doesn't love it when you make a mess." Esther paused. "She had a hard day with Ruth today, though. Oh, poor Ruth, she had three accidents, dirty ones."

"Well, she has to expect that kind of thing if she adopts kids," Roger said.

"Maybe she's... maybe she doesn't want to adopt us. Maybe she's asking Uncle Robert to take us."

Roger and Esther stared at Robert. "Really?" Roger said.

"No, no, I'm sure that isn't it," Esther said. "Robert, how could you scare Roger so? She would have told us."

"Maybe not," Robert said. "It isn't like she asked us before agreeing to take us; maybe she figures it would be 'more efficient' if she just wrote Uncle Robert on her own."

"No, no, I'm sure that isn't it," Esther protested, her eyes starting to water again.

"Well, who is she writing, then?" Robert asked.

"I don't know. Maybe it is Uncle Robert or one of the other uncles. Maybe it's Uncle Roger. And she's crying because she's telling him how we are doing, and that reminds her of..." she glanced at Roger... "of other things, and they make her cry."

"I could try to eat less," Roger said.

"We could try not to get in fights," Robert said. "I don't think any number of lickings is going to stop Geoffrey from being mad at us, but I can try to, you know, turn the other cheek?"

"Like which cheek you fall on when he knocks you down?" Roger asked, and Robert pushed him, grinning.

"Well, we should all try to be good," Esther said decidedly. "I know she acts all super strong and all, but it can't be easy having us. I burn the cooking, Roger eats too much..."

"I still can't do all the milking on my own," Robert said.

"Anyway, we should all try to do better," Esther said and, with a quick wipe of her face, walked back out the door.

Strawberry Pie Ingredients

The course of true love never did run smooth."
— ***William Shakespeare,***

Chapter Nine

THE ADDITION

E sther and Ruth were having a very fun time working on pot pie crusts. A very fun time. Aunt Grace had set Ruth to 'mixing' the dough, and Esther was taking the dough and shaping it, rolling it out and cutting the edges, then taking the extra she had cut off and giving it back to Ruth for more 'mixing'. Which Esther had to be careful not to use because it would be tough.

"Who is that?" she heard, and she and Ruth went to the window to see a wagon coming down the drive toward the house. "Oh, botheration! It is Jonathon... Mr Thacker." Aunt Grace said. "You girls go into the parlour and wait there. When the boys come down from their room, you have them wait there, too."

Esther picked up Ruth and went to the parlour, then decided to tell the boys right away. She put Ruth down and raced up the stairs. "Boys, someone is coming and Aunt Grace wants us to not go into the kitchen, but to wait in the parlour!"

"What, why?" asked Roger, pulling on his shirt, and the two boys followed her quickly down the stairs.

"Afternoon, Mrs Livingston," they heard a loud, male voice say from the kitchen.

"Good afternoon, Jonathon," Aunt Grace replied, sounding annoyed. "And to what do we owe the pleasure of this visit?"

"I reckon you already know," the voice drawled. "After my wife died two years ago, I came by and asked you to take her place. Our land is right next to each other, and your dairy and my hay fields will go well together, as will you and I."

"And I told you at that time that I had no need of a husband!"

"Well, that was then, and this is now. When I heard that you had gotten yourself four young'ens, I said to myself, well, that they needed a father. Can't argue with that."

There was a pause, a very long pause in Esther's ears, and then Aunt Grace said, in a very subdued tone, "Well, I don't see how we can marry. There simply isn't room; the girls sleep with me in my room."

"So, that's your only objection? That there isn't room?"

There was another very long pause. "Well, yes. I can't really argue with your reasoning otherwise. I hadn't intended to have these four children, but now that they are here, well, you make a powerful argument. They do need a father, I can't argue with that. They had the most wonderful father before..."

"... but, as I say, I don't have room," Aunt Grace concluded, her voice getting firm and decisive again.

"Well, if that's all of your objection, I'll be over tomorrow afternoon."

"What, why?"

"I'll be bringing supplies by. I been thinking ever since I heard about these new young'ens, and I drew up plans last night for an addition to your house. I'll bring the supplies by tomorrow, and the next day, you tell your boys to be ready to help me on Wednesday after school."

Aunt Grace didn't answer. The door banged, and they all rushed to the window and saw the wagon driving away. Esther, thinking quickly, thrust Ruth into Robert's arms. "Take her with you to the creek. I need to talk to Aunt Grace."

Robert and Roger left, and Ruth, looking a bit confused, but not upset, and Esther marched with Esther off to the kitchen.

Aunt Grace was standing in the middle of the kitchen, looking... well, not looking at all like Aunt Grace. She took one look at Esther's face, "You heard? Well, obviously, you heard. I should have sent you outside. These walls aren't near thick enough for his voice, and I wasn't speaking so quietly myself. Well, there it is then, you know. And the boys?"

Esther nodded.

"Well, best they do, I suppose. They will need to learn to... that he will be the new man of our house."

"You're going to marry him, then?"

"You heard, didn't you? I only put forward one objection, and he answered it. He is perfectly correct. I was probably foolish not to marry him before, but his wife was a good friend of mine, in her way, and I couldn't see replacing her."

"But, but it sounds like he is just after your dairy!"

"That is not what he said at all. He made the perfectly valid point that his hay business, plus our dairy business, would go very well together. And they certainly will do. I'm sure that Robert can tell you how much of a benefit it will be to us to get our hay free, as it were. We buy it from him now, which is quite a burden."

"But you can't marry him just for that!"

"Don't be silly, child. We are both too old to be snatched away with some foolish romantic dreams. He has a very

good business and naturally wants a wife. I have no particular desire for a husband, but there is nothing wrong with
him, and he is perfectly right; this house needs a man in it.
Robert is doing an excellent job, but he isn't fully of age and
hasn't come into his full strength. There are a lot of jobs
that he and I would have to do together, or that we would
have to hire a man to come do, that Mr Thacker will do
quite easily. Now, get back to your pie crusts. Where is
Ruth?"

"I sent her off with the boys to the creek so we could
talk," Esther said, turning back to the table.

"Ah, well, that was wise. Anyway, I think we have talked
about it quite enough."

Roger did not fully understand why Mr Thacker was going to
be building something onto their house. His aunt's house, he
quickly corrected. He, and his siblings, would soon be going
back to live with their mother and father.

Anyway, he didn't understand it, but that didn't make it
any less fun. Mr Thacker had delivered three more large piles
of lumber in the morning while they were at school, and
Roger, his dinner and afternoon chores and reading all done,
had raced out to see what kind of fun he could have with
them.

He went up to the smaller boards... long but smaller... and
climbed up them. This was fun. He could see for, well, for a
distance. Not as much as from his room or the attic gables.

He went over to the pile of thicker boards, wondering
what they were for. Then he went to the next pile, which was
several rather large stones. Whitish stones...

"Working hard, Bobtail?" he heard and spun to see
Geoffrey coming up.

"None your business," he said, backing up, but Geoffrey ignored him and came over to the stones.

Roger stared at him. Geoffrey had never, ever come over to their house before. And, after the big fight on Sunday, none of the scholars had even talked to him all day at school, and even the teacher hadn't called on him. Nor had he talked to anyone, but had spent the whole day frowning at everyone. It was the first time Roger had ever been in a fight without getting a licking. He had heard from Carl that Geoffrey had not only gotten a licking, but two lectures!

Roger watched Geoffrey. He was tempted to run play, but he was hoping that Geoffrey knew what the stones were there for.

"Hello, Geoffrey," he heard and spun to see Robert coming up, a stern look on his face. He saw Esther looking from the window, a worried look on her face.

"Hey Bob," Geoffrey said. "What you doing here? You look too scrawny to lay footers."

Roger spun back to the pile of stone. Footers? What were they?

He had a thought and ran back to the house and peered around. Sure enough, under the house, there were stones all in a line at the bottom, holding up the house.

Roger heard Mr Thacker's wagon coming and spun around. Sure enough, he and his wagon were coming down their driveway. Aunt Grace's driveway. With more stones.

All three boys watched the wagon drive in. "Good thing you boys are here," Mr Thacker said. "You big boys help get these stones down... ones you can lift. You, Little Boy, you come here."

Roger ran over, but Geoffrey started to edge away. Mr Thacker turned, "Did you hear me, boy?"

"Yes, sir," Geoffrey said. "But my clothes..." he indicated his clothes, which were all fancy. Roger was glad he didn't have to run around in clothes like that, always worrying about getting them dirty or ripped or whatever.

"You look about this boy's size," Mr Thacker said to Geoffrey. "You, Little Boy, take him up and have him put on some of Big Boy's clothes. You, let me show you where to put the stones."

Geoffrey glared at Roger, who grinned back and led Geoffrey into the house and upstairs. "I don't know why I have to help," Geoffrey said while the two climbed up the steps.

"He asked you to."

"Is this your room?" Geoffrey asked when Roger opened the door.

"Yup."

"And Bob?"

"Yup."

"But where do you sleep?"

"Couch," Roger said. Geoffrey had undressed, and Roger handed him an old set of Robert's denims and an old shirt.

"These are disgusting," Geoffrey said, pulling them on.

"They'll be worse when we're done, I reckon."

"Well, there is that," Geoffrey agreed.

Back outside, Geoffrey went to help Robert move stones, and Mr Thacker called Roger over to hold the other end of some string while he pounded stakes.

"Now, we're going to dig," Mr Thacker announced, pulling shovels
and picks from off the wagon. "We'll have a race. You big boys will each take a side, and Little Boy and I will take the long end."

Roger was not very happy to

be called 'Little Boy,' but very glad that he would be on the same team as Mr Thacker.

"Little Boy!" Mr Thacker said after Roger's third shovelful went flying. "You have to be more organised. Make a nice row of dirt all along here."

Roger noticed that the other boys changed the way they were doing their dirt and didn't know why he had to be the one to get yelled at.

Mr Thacker seemed to spend most of his time going over to the big boys, or Roger, and telling them or showing them how to dig, how to arrange the dirt, how deep to dig, how to make the walls... but he and Roger still managed to get ahead on their long ditch more than the other boys were doing on theirs.

"Well, that's enough for now," he said, wiping his brow. "Let's see how you two boys did."

Mr Thacker took a measuring rope out of his wagon and went over to where Robert stood, sweating and covered in dirt. He reached down and used the string to measure Robert's hole. "Four feet long. Good job, Big Boy."

Then he went over to Geoffery, who was cleaner but still very dirty. "Three foot ten inches," he said, and Geoffrey flushed. But then Mr Thacker put his rope down the hole. "One and a half feet," he said, then went over to Robert. "One foot four inches."

Geoffrey at first looked confused and then grinned. "Well, I'll call that a tie," Mr Thacker said. "Little boy and I won, but I think we all deserve a prize."

Mr Thacker walked over to his wagon, and Roger followed him, eager to figure out what the treat was. But Robert and Geoffrey stood and looked very tired. "I suppose you all like fudge?" Mr Thacker asked, pulling a package out from under the wagon bench, and the bigger boys suddenly found the energy to race over.

"Eat it now before the women folk see," he said, and Roger, looking nervously around for Aunt Grace, crammed his into his mouth.

"OK, now all three of you go rinse off, and you, Preacher's Kid, you tell your father I want you here every day after dinner like this. You hear?"

"Yes, sir," Geoffrey said, sounding like he wanted to cry.

"Go now," Mr Thacker said, and the boys raced off to the pump.

A few minutes later, upstairs, all of them pulling their clothes on, Geoffrey looked at Robert. "Did you put him up to this?"

"Me?" Robert said. "Up to what?"

"Making me come over and work."

"Fudge was good," Roger said.

Geoffrey paused, "Well, yes, the fudge was good. But I don't want to come over and work with you lot. I'm a preacher's kid!"

"Well, feel free to tell Mr Thacker that," Robert said.

"Like he would care. Common farmer, what does he know."

"He knows he told you to tell your father that you were supposed to come, and if you don't show up then he'll go and ask him where you are. Then you'll get a licking, sure."

"Well, I don't know what I am to wear. I don't have clothes for this kind of messy work."

"You can wear those again," Roger said, pointing to the clothes Geoffrey had thrown on the floor. "Esther will wash them, or Aunt Grace. Better wear better shoes, though. Don't you have no work boots?"

"What business is it of yours, Bobtail?"

"None my business. Only this work will be hard on those shoes."

"I have my old pair," Robert said. "If you think they would fit."

Geoffrey turned red. "I don't want..." he looked down at his shoes. "I can't keep... very well, let me see them."

Robert got out his old pair of shoes, which weren't work boots, but which were so worn out it wouldn't matter, and (although Robert didn't say so) had grown just a bit small for him.

Geoffrey pulled them on with a disgusted look on his face. Then he stood up, walked around a few steps, and took them back off. "Very well, I suppose they will do."

He started out the door and Roger yelled after him, "See you tomorrow!"

Robert turned and rolled his eyes at him, and then, hearing the door slam downstairs, the two of them collapsed in giggles.

"Very good, boys," Mr Thacker said, and Robert grinned. He was very, very glad they were done digging the ditch.

"Now, Preacher's Kid, you're from around here. Can you tell me why we dug this ditch?"

Robert and Roger both looked at Geoffrey, who flushed. "Footings."

"True, but a little more explanation would be nice."

"You're going to lay those rocks in the hole, all put together like, and use that as what the house, or the addition, will sit on."

"That is what we are going to do," Mr Thacker corrected. "Little boy, I want you down in the ditch to help balance and move the rocks. Big Boy, you will start out as the fetcher while I teach Preacher's Kid how to lay."

Robert thought Geoffrey would be upset, but he didn't seem upset. He didn't move very quickly, but he kept his face forward like he was interested. He listened to the explanation of which rock to begin with, which Robert didn't really understand, except it had to be a big one, and was going to go in the corner.

"Which you should know about, being a preacher's son," Mr Thacker said. "You know the verses about the cornerstone."

Geoffrey flushed but nodded. "So we need a large stone, Big Boy," Mr Thacker said to Robert, and Robert looked around.

"This one?" He asked, seeing one that was larger than its neighbours.

"Keep looking," Mr Thacker said, "Bigger than that."

"Oh, one of these," he said a minute later, finding two rocks, each almost double the size of all the other rocks.

"Yes. Now, Preacher's Kid, he will need help lifting it."

The two boys struggled across the yard and then Mr Thacker helped them put it in the ditch. "We might as well get the next one in," he said, and the two boys went back for it.

Then Mr Thacker explained to Geoffrey what the next stone needed to look like, and Robert found one like that and handed it down. Geoffrey and Roger put it in place while Robert looked for the next rock.

An hour later, the three boys were moving and placing rocks down in their ditch without any help, and Geoffrey was even coming up to help Robert when the rock he chose was too large.

Mr Thacker was working on the other side, choosing and laying his own stones.

"Good job, boys!" Mr Thacker said a while later, and the three boys looked up. They were filthy, as the rocks hadn't been exactly clean, and they were so heavy that the boys had to carry them pretty close to the chest. And naturally, Roger had felt perfectly free to squirm about in the ditch to help 'get the rock exactly right.'

"Fudge?" Roger said, leaping out of the ditch.

"No," Mr Thacker said, and his face fell. "Pie. I stopped by the store..."

But Roger was already racing to the wagon and came back proudly carrying a pail, which he handed to Mr Thacker. "Mrs Jones, at the general store, baked a pie today, and I asked her for a piece for me and three big pieces for the three big boys that were helping me. And some of her bottled ginger beer. Which is back in the wagon, Little Boy."

Roger raced off and came back with four bottles of ginger beer. Mr Thacker handed them out to the boys, took one himself along with a slice of pie... and the four of them sat on the lumber eating contentedly.

"I will see you all tomorrow," he said, after a few minutes' silence, and went and got in his wagon.

Robert got up soon after and started toward the pump, but stopped when he saw Geoffrey had gone, instead, to the ditch. He went back and stood next to him. "Pretty good, eh?"

"I can't believe we did that," Geoffrey answered and then, seeming to realise that he was talking to Robert, stalked off toward the pump.

"Jonathon!"

Esther and Ruth had been sitting with the boys. Mr Thacker had brought a hot cobbler, and he said that because they had brought out the bowls and spoons to eat it with, that she and Ruth could have some. Which Esther thought silly... but the cobbler was good.

Aunt Grace was standing there and turned toward Mr Thacker. "Jonathon!" she said. "We aren't married yet!"

"Getting there," he said, patting her on the shoulder and walking away.

"What did he do?" Esther asked.

"Pinched her bottom," Geoffrey said, grinning. "And she didn't even slap him."

Robert laughed, and Esther frowned at him. "Robert, you know that isn't proper."

"Well, Mr Thacker isn't always proper," Robert said. "Although I don't know why that isn't proper."

"What do you mean he isn't always proper?" Esther said. "It isn't like you know him, just working with him these few days."

"I knew him before that," Robert said. "He's part of my cheese run."

"And he does improper things?" she asked, scandalised.

"Well... funny things, anyway. He has this board up on this pole, with circles and everything on it, and every time I am there, he makes me chuck a rock at it. He keeps track of my score and all. Said he did it with all of his boys, kept their wrists in shape or something."

"Well, I don't know that that is improper," Esther said, after thinking about it. "It is odd, certainly. But Aunt Grace said that he shouldn't have done..." she blushed, "... what he did."

"Girls is always saying that," Geoffrey said. "Around here, anyway. My ma is always telling my pa he shouldn't... oh, hush, they're coming," he said, and busied himself with his cobbler.

Esther did her best to keep her eyes down on her own dessert, which she had largely finished, but she made the mistake of glancing up and caught Aunt Grace's eyes. Why, she was blushing! Aunt Grace was blushing!

"I like Mr Thacker," Roger declared, helping himself to some more mashed potatoes.

"Well, I should hope so," Aunt Grace said, with a bit of a frown.

"But you don't like him," he said, and she reddened.

"Roger! How could you say such a thing!"

Roger paused, his spoon halfway to his mouth. He looked wildly back and forth from Esther to Aunt Grace. "But I, umm, I thought..."

But Aunt Grace was no longer looking at him. "Esther? What kind of nonsense have you been telling Roger?"

Esther burst into tears and ran out of the room, causing Roger's eyes to bug out of his head.

"If you will excuse us," Aunt Grace said to Robert. "Roger, come with us."

Roger followed Aunt Grace out of the room, his backside already tingling. But, instead of going to the woodshed, they went upstairs. Up the stairs and into Aunt Grace's room, where Esther lay on the bed, her face buried in the sheets, sobbing. Or, at least, crying. Roger never did understand the difference. He didn't cry or sob.

"Now, Esther, sit up and apologise to Roger."

Roger's mouth dropped open. Was Esther supposed to apologise to him? What for?

"But, but... I thought you didn't like him," Esther said. "I mean... he isn't at all proper! And he asked you to marry him for two whole years, and you always said no, and he's so old...!"

"Now Esther, I told you why that was. Now you explain it to Roger. I can't have the boy thinking I don't even like the man I will be marrying, and we will be living with and all."

Esther sat up, dried her tears, hiccuped a few times, cried

a bit more, and dried her tears again. "Well, Roger. It isn't that Aunt Grace doesn't like Mr Thacker. I shouldn't have said that. He isn't at all proper, so I thought... I thought it would be hard for Aunt Grace to live with him."

"Certainly, it will be hard. But we do hard things in life, and that doesn't mean I don't like him. Or love him either, although I don't usually speak in such a way."

"So, anyway, Roger... Mr Thacker asked Aunt Grace to marry him when his wife died. His first wife that had his children. And Aunt Grace said no."

"Which was silly of me, Roger. Even grown women can be silly. My life these past years would have been very different if I had said yes."

Esther watched Aunt Grace as if hoping she would say more, but when she didn't, Esther went on. "She said no because, well, Mr Thacker isn't always an easy man. And because Mr Thacker's wife was her friend and so she didn't think she could take her place. And..." Esther looked at Aunt Grace, who nodded.

"And you know, Roger, that Aunt Grace never had any children with her first husband. And she thought that Mr Thacker wanted more children..."

"I'm sure he does. And a fine father he is, too. Even with you lot, he's starting already."

"So... so she wasn't sure that he really wanted to marry her, or if he was just, well, their lands are touching, and all, and they knew each other, so it would have been easy..."

"But now, Roger," Aunt Grace said. "I realised how silly I was. It wasn't my job to tell him what kind of wife he wanted, or whether... anyway, it wasn't my job. What my job is now, and I intend to do a good job of it, I can assure you, is to be a good wife and to do a good job taking care of you all."

"That won't mean it will be easy, or that everything he wants will come easy to me, but I intend to do a good job regardless. You just ignore any little bumps on the road and concentrate on the destination."

So saying, she got up and clumped off downstairs, loudly.

"So... so she likes him?" Roger asked Esther.

"Oh, yes... she even loves him... in her way. But it isn't easy, when a husband dies, to start to think of another man in that way. That's what she is always telling me."

"So why did you tell me she doesn't like him?"

"Oh, because it will be hard for her! And I don't want... she's already done so much for us, and he said... you remember... he said she had to marry him because of us!"

"But... I don't understand."

"Oh, I don't either. But it was wrong of me to tell you that she didn't like him. Very wrong, and I will try not to do it again, and we must never let Ruth think that!"

"Ruth likes him," Roger said.

"Certainly she does. We all do. Now go eat; I'm going to cry some more."

Roger fled at that. Girls were strange.

Roger was up in a tree, eating an apple, which is how he got to see Geoffrey coming before anyone else. Robert and Mr Thacker were still discussing the worship lesson, which Roger didn't even understand what they were saying, so he came out to climb a tree and wait for afternoon work.

So he got to see Geoffrey coming, and boy did he look mad! Not even mad-frustrated like he had been the first couple of days. He looked mad-mad, like yell-at-you mad. Or even hit-you mad. And he had a sack he was carrying. Like a sack to carry clothes in, like they had had on the train when they came here.

"Hey!" he yelled when Geoffrey got close. Couldn't get hit way up here.

Geoffrey looked startled, looked around, and finally looked up in the tree. "Aren't we working today?" he asked.

"Sure," Roger said, "Just waiting for you. Something about learning to measure and cut and all. I'm supposed to hold the other end of the string."

He hit the ground and walked near, but not too near, Geoffrey, who didn't look quite so mad. "What you got in the sack?" Roger asked.

"Clothes!" Geoffrey snapped. "My father says I'm to spend the night tonight and tomorrow and go to church with you Bobtails. Here, Little Boy, take my sack up to your room."

Roger figured it was Geoffrey's job to take his own sack upstairs, but he didn't figure it was worth getting him mad when he was already mad, so he grabbed the sack and rushed upstairs.

When he got downstairs and back outside, the other two boys were standing with Mr Thacker, who was talking about how to measure. "Come here, Little Boy," Mr Thacker said, and Roger grinned and ran over. "Take this string and hold this end with the stick on it hard against this beam."

He watched to make sure that Roger had it firm against the beam and, unrolling the string from the spool, walked across the construction to another beam. "Now, Preacher's Kid, this will be your job. You have Little Boy hold the string... and you watch him, mind, Preacher's Kid, this job is your responsibility... and then you come over here..."

Roger ignored Geoffrey's job and listened to the geese flying overhead. At least, he thought they were geese, making honk-honk noises. That was what geese did, wasn't it?

"Robert?" Aunt Grace yelled, and Robert, with an apologetic look at Mr Thacker, ran off, and was soon off in the buggy.

"Where's he going?" Geoffrey asked.

"Cheese deliveries," Roger said.

"Back to your job, Preacher's Kid," Mr Thacker said, and Geoffrey, frowning, went back to measuring.

It was two hours later when Robert came back in the buggy. Aunt Grace went out to meet him, and he came hurrying back. "Sorry," he said to Mr Thacker, "I had deliveries to make."

"That's your job," Mr Thacker said, "No need to apologise."

"Are we almost done?" Geoffrey asked.

"Not even close," Mr Thacker said, and he groaned.

"Very well, we can take it out to the boys now," Aunt Grace said. "I will carry the pot; it is very heavy. Do you bring the bowls. Ruth, you will carry the spoons."

Aunt Grace picked up the pot and walked out the kitchen door. Esther hurriedly got some spoons out of the drawer and gave them to Ruth, then climbed up and got down some bowls, then hurried over to the door and held it open for Ruth, who toddled after her carrying the spoons quite proudly all the way over to a fire that the boys had started. And they had put big boards around it to sit on.

"Well, what have you made for us, Big Girl?" Mr Thacker said, coming up and clapping her on the back.

"Chicken and dumplings," Esther said proudly. "We worked on it all afternoon."

"Well, sit down and join us," Mr Thacker said. "I'll pray, and you can tell us all about it."

Everyone, even Aunt Grace, sat down quickly and Mr

Thacker prayed. "So, Big Girl, tell us how you make chicken and dumplings. I've always wondered."

"Well, I've never made it before," Esther admitted. "But the way Aunt Grace does it is she takes some chickens and bakes them... we made several so we could have some cold chicken for later, some other day. We baked them with salt, and pepper, and some other spices on it."

"Then, after they are baked, we took the stuff that came down..."

"The drippings," Aunt Grace said.

"The drippings, and we put them in a pot with a whole bunch of vegetables."

"Which ones, Esther?" Aunt Grace asked.

"Onions... and carrots... and... and celery. And garlic."

"Which we treat as a spice," Aunt Grace said.

"And we boiled them a long time, and had to add water several times. While they were boiling, we deboned the chicken once it had cooled."

"Then we made up the dumplings and, just before we put them in, we put a whole bunch of the chicken in, then put the dumplings in and then, after a few minutes, brought it out here!" She finished triumphantly.

"And it's great!" Roger said, waving his spoon around.

"Thank you, Roger," Aunt Grace said. "Now, what did you do today? I'm sure Ruth would like to know."

Roger looked at Ruth, his mouth open, but then said, "We are still working on the beams. We need to get them..." he looked at Ruth again, then turned toward the house and pointed, "Ruthy, we need to get all of those big boards up, so they will make the shape of the new part of the house."

Ruth looked at the house, looked at Roger, and took another bite.

"But what did you do, Roger?" Aunt Grace asked.

"I held string. Measuring string. I held one end, and

Geoffrey held the other and figured out how long it was supposed to be."

"Ah, I'm sure that was helpful. And you'll be spending the night with us, Geoffrey?"

Geoffrey, who had been grinning while stuffing himself with the chicken and dumplings, frowned but said politely enough, "Yes, ma'am. My father said as how we would be working all tonight and tomorrow and as how I should spend the night here."

"Well, I'll let the boys settle you in their room. It is very kind of you to come and work."

Geoffrey turned beet red, "Thank you, ma'am."

"Before you go off to bed, we need to do our evening worship. Little Boy, run off and get the Bible, please," Mr Thacker said, and Roger put his bowl and spoon down and darted off, coming back seconds later with the Bible.

"Very good. Now, I should warn all of you, I will have questions for you after I read the text. Especially you, Preacher's Kid. We will be counting on you."

"Yes, sir," Geoffrey said, again beet red.

"Which will start with our very first verse. Hard verse, I've always said. *'John 1, In the beginning was the word, and the word was with God, and the word was God.'* Now that's a bit confusing. Who does it say is God?"

He was staring at Geoffrey, who gulped, but answered bravely enough, "That verse says that the word, who was Jesus, was both with God and was God. It's part of the doctrine of the trinity..."

They all listened to Geoffrey, who talked for quite a while, and then, when he stopped, Mr Thacker nodded.

"That's about what I thought. Good explanation. Now our Big Boy will be next..."

Robert answered the next question, and then Roger, and then Mr Thacker went back to

Geoffrey. Esther was glad he wasn't asking her any of these questions! Although Roger's questions were easier.

"Well, that's enough for tonight, I think," Mr Thacker said. Roger was almost disappointed. He had liked his questions, although he hadn't much understood the questions he had asked the bigger boys. "I will pray, and then you, Little Boy, take Preacher's Kid up to your room, and the two of you get to sleep. I will be going over the plans with Big Boy here."

Well, Roger didn't like that idea! After the prayer, Roger stood and waited for Geoffrey, who reluctantly got up and came after him.

"I don't see why Robert gets to stay up and go over the plans," he complained. "Aren't I doing the same work?"

"Not willingly," Roger said, proud to use the big word.

"Still doing it, aren't I?"

"Doing good," Roger admitted. "Good to have you. Would go slower without you."

That seemed to shut Geoffrey up, and neither one said a word until they were up in their room. "Where am I going to sleep?" he asked, and Roger spun around the room, his brain very busy.

If he put him in the bed with Robert, which the bed was plenty big enough for two boys if they slept head to tail, then they would fight. But the couch was Roger's! But what would mother say about being hospitable...?

"The couch," Roger said, making the sacrifice.

"Oh. Well. Isn't that where you sleep?"

"I will manage a couple of nights with Robert," Roger said, rummaging around to find his nightshirt and pulling it on.

"Oh, well, umm, thank you."

Roger knelt and said his prayers, then got in and waited while Geoffrey made up the couch (very neatly!), said his own prayers, lay down with his face against the couch and...

Roger figured he was asleep and crept out of bed. He could hear Esther and Aunt Grace still working in the kitchen, and Robert and Mr Thacker had just come in from outside and gone into the parlour. Roger snuck downstairs where, luckily, they had left the parlour door open.

"These are the plans for the addition," Mr Thacker was saying, and Roger wished he could be there to see! "The addition will be six feet wide and twenty feet long, as we have already measured. It will go up for both stories and the attic, although that part of the attic will be slightly shorter than the rest so that we don't have to redo the upper roof."

Roger heard a slight noise and looked to see Geoffrey sitting carefully down next to him. Oh, well.

"On the ground floor, the addition will be touching, as I'm sure you know, the kitchen and what is now the dining room. We will be switching the dining room and the parlour, so it will end up being the parlour that gets bigger."

Roger heard some paper rustle, "But we won't just be knocking out the wall?"

"That's correct. We won't be knocking out either wall; we will be making an opening between them. In the kitchen, it will be either a door or a very thick curtain; we will need to discuss it with your aunt. In the parlour, we are going to make an arch..."

Roger heard the door from the kitchen open and, quick as a wink, raced back up the stairs, Geoffrey right behind him.

Then he heard Esther talking to Ruth as she brought her upstairs. Then he heard them go into the girls' bedroom, and he heard a distinct mumble, no doubt Esther getting Ruth undressed and saying her prayers with her. Then he heard his door open and felt a presence, and he opened one eye to look.

Esther was at the door, looking at him. She looked over to where Geoffrey was on the couch, looked back at Roger, winked, and left. She could be OK, Esther.

Esther stood at the window, watching the boys. She didn't know why Geoffrey came. He never looked happy when he came, especially when he came back downstairs with Robert's old clothes on... which Esther washed frantically each evening. Once, he had had to come downstairs to find them hanging in the kitchen, still drying.

But after an hour or so working, he always seemed to cheer up and, until after the boys ate whatever special thing Mr Thacker brought for them, stayed cheerful. He didn't seem to like spending the night, but he really seemed to enjoy their meals. She felt sorry for him having to eat at his house.

"Mommy?" she heard, and turned to see Ruth coming up to her. Her heart broke. She shouldn't be calling her that, but she couldn't yell at her for it—poor dear.

"Yes, Ruthy?"

"Apple?"

"Yes, Dear, I'll get you an apple." Living here was amazing; Aunt Grace never set the slightest bounds on what you could eat. Roger was in heaven.

"Where boys?" Ruth asked when she had her apple and had taken the first bite.

"Out in the yard, working with Mr Thacker," Esther said, and Ruth toddled off to the parlour, where she heard a chair scraping along the floor. She put the pot pie she was working on in the oven—Roger loved pot pie—and peeked into the parlour where Ruth had pulled up a chair to the window and stood on it, watching the boys.

She had just put the second pot pie in the oven when the kitchen door banged open, and three wet boys came streaking through the kitchen and up the stairs. Roger was the first down and came into the kitchen to peek into the oven.

"Pot pie," Esther said. "What were you boys doing today?"

"Beams," he said. "Lots of really careful measuring and sawing. Two big boys on the saw. I couldn't do much except hold string and pick up scraps and things, but I still got the treat: fudge again."

"I would say it would spoil your appetite, but nothing seems to spoil *your* appetite."

"Not for pot pies, it doesn't. Are they any good?"

"I certainly hope so. I boiled down the chicken, and Aunt Grace helped me with the white sauce before she went back to the barn."

"I thought pot pies had a brown sauce."

"It is called a white sauce, but it gets brown from the chicken," she said. "What will you be doing tomorrow?"

"More beams," Roger said. "Both stories and then up to the attic."

"I don't understand... hello Robert... I don't understand what kind of room you are building."

"It's not exactly a room down here," Robert said. "Mr Thacker is calling it an 'extension'. It's six more feet along the whole side of the house. Downstairs, it will make the kitchen and the dining room bigger, except we're going to switch the dining room with the parlour, so it will be the parlour that will get bigger. He's bringing lots more bookshelves, which will all go in this section, making kind of a library."

"That will be good. And upstairs?"

"Upstairs, he's building your room, you and Ruth. He says as how you can't sleep with them once he moves in."

"But... what kind of room will it be?"

"A long, skinny room on the other side of ours. Six feet wide and the whole house long. He says he's going to build shelves all along the side wall for you to put things on since there won't be much room for wardrobes and things, with your two beds and all. He has a regular bed for Ruth. Your door will be in our room."

Esther couldn't quite imagine the room, but she guessed it would do. Certainly, she wouldn't want to sleep in the same room with Mr Thacker, although she would miss Aunt Grace.

Success is the ability to continue to move through total disaster.
— ***Winston Churchill***

Chapter Ten

SUCCESS

"Esther, go down into the cool room and get me two pounds of salt pork from the small crock."

"Yes, ma'am," Esther said and, grabbing a bowl to carry the pork in, went downstairs. Wondering, the whole time, why she needed to get two whole pounds of pork. They had been feeding Mr Thacker and Geoffrey, both of whom could eat, for four weeks now, and they rarely needed more than one pound of salt pork. It wasn't a meat that one ate in great amounts... almost more of a spice!

"Now, get out two of our larger dutch ovens and start them heating. Then cut the meat into small cubes."

"Yes, ma'am. Should I put lard in the bottom of the ovens?"

"Yes, quite right. Then divide the meat into two portions and start them frying. While they fry, cut some onions... about equal portions."

"What are we making?" Esther asked, lugging one of the ovens over to the stove and setting it on. Mother would never have allowed her to do this.

"Baked beans," Aunt Grace said. "I'll be getting out some beans I canned before you came here."

Esther cut and fried and cut and fried, fascinated with the recipe, but still confused. It seemed like they were making an awful lot of beans! Perhaps Aunty wanted some for another meal.

"Now we will add some molasses," Aunt Grace said... "Oh, dear, run up and get Ruth, please."

Esther ran upstairs and grabbed Ruth, hurrying back down. "Look, Ruth, we are making baked beans!" she said when they made it back to the kitchen.

"Taste?" Ruth asked.

"Not yet, Ruth dear," Aunt Grace said. "We need to let the tastes settle. Now do your job and take water to the boys."

Ruth wiggled, and Esther set her down. She hurried to the door, grabbed a leather bottle that Aunt kept full there, and darted outside. She had grown so used to doing these jobs! Practically every day Esther learned, often from Ruth, about some new job Ruth had while Esther and the boys were away at school.

"Now, we need to get to that cheese we put up yesterday," Aunt Grace said. "It needs wax..."

Four hours later, Esther was exhausted. Cheesemaking was a lot of work! Ruth had run in and out several times for new water, and, the last time, they had all tasted the baked beans, which were marvellous.

"Mommy, wagon coming!" Ruth said, banging in the kitchen door and running up to Aunt Grace.

"Oh, good. Go out and greet them, Ruth, Esther."

Greet who? Esther wondered, but went out the back door. Aunt Grace didn't favour children asking questions that they could easily find the answer to themselves, which she could do by going out and seeing.

She looked down the road and, sure enough, a wagon was coming... why, it was Geoffrey's family! All in their wagon together, with Lilly and Carl and the others... the baby busy on the mother's breast.

She was tempted to run down the road, but Aunty would never approve of behaviour like that, so she waited until the wagon stopped, and Esther ran up to it, "Hello!" she said. "Welcome!"

"Thank you, my dear," the preacher said, stepping down from his wagon. "Something smells wonderful."

Esther's heart gave a little leap then realised that they must have come for dinner!

"Hello Esther," Lilly said from where she was helping one of her little siblings down. Carl had already run off to the addition and was climbing up next to Roger, who was greeting him loudly.

At first she worried about Carl's clothes, but then she realised that he had play clothes on. Indeed the whole family except for the mother were dressed very casually. The mother was dressed in a fancy dress... although having the bodice open and the baby at the breast kind of spoiled the effect. She had heard (Lilly had told her) that Geoffrey's mother tried to do her nursing at home, but was most frustrated that this babe would not keep to such a schedule and almost always insisted, loudly, on nursing in the middle of pretty much every event. Lilly thought the whole thing very funny and said she wouldn't mind nursing her baby anywhere!

"Father?" She heard and turned to see Geoffrey coming over to them, his eyes wide with shock.

"We've come to see your work," the preacher said. "Mr Thacker invited us. This is the addition?"

Geoffrey turned, grinning. "Yes, Father. It is six feet big on this side and..."

"Well, so you've come," Mr Thacker said, coming up and shaking the preacher's hand.

"Yes, yes, we wanted to see what our son was doing."

"Well, this is what he was doing—doing a good job, too. He's lazy but not stupid. I've had him..."

"Lazy?" Geoffrey's mother said. "I am not accustomed to... how dare you...."

"He's right, Mother." Geoffrey said, and Esther and his mother both looked at him in shock. "Now, let us show you what we've done, Father..."

Esther did her best not to stare at Geoffrey's mother as she stood there, her mouth open, staring after her son as he led his father over to the addition.

Esther felt someone come up behind her and heard Lilly whisper, "What are you cooking?"

"Come see," Esther said, glad to get out of the awkward situation, and Lilly and her little sister followed her into the kitchen.

They were just lifting the lid off of the first pot when Aunt Grace said, "Good. Girls, take them out to the fire that the boys started, we'll be eating outside, and the coals will finish cooking them nicely."

Lilly looked a bit askance at the size of the pot, so Esther lifted it down, and the two girls struggled outside, Lilly's sister holding the door.

They were setting the oven down when Lilly's father, who was sitting next to Mr Thacker on the logs by the fire, both of them looking the other way at the addition, asked, "So, how is your plan working?"

"Bang up!" Mr Thacker said. "They glared at each other like rival cats the first few days, but working together, bathing together, your poor son having to wear Robert's clothes, all got them together. Won't say your son is the most friendly boy I've ever come across, but he's polite and obedient with me and works well with Robert. Works smart, not hard... too lazy to do otherwise.

"But we got those boys together now. Don't think they'll be bickering after this. I started our first day calling your kid 'Preacher's Kid' just to... Esther?"

Esther flushed, and she and Lilly fled back to the house. She hadn't meant to, but they had been eavesdropping!

But to think, Mr Thacker and Lilly's father had done all this on purpose! Even to him calling Geoffrey 'Preacher's Kid'. And, she supposed, always calling the others by their roles'... 'Big Boy' and 'Little Boy'... which Roger now loved, and even 'Big Girl', which Esther didn't mind, and 'Little Girl,' which Ruth accepted without thought. She supposed he called them that so he could call Geoffrey 'Preacher's Kid' without him suspecting.

The boys were laying in bed, each with their own book, when Geoffrey, from the couch, said, "Listen to this poem, I have no idea what it means, but it sounds deep."

The Gods of the Copybook Headings

As I pass through my incarnations in every age and race,
I make my proper prostrations to the Gods of the Market Place.
Peering through reverent fingers I watch them flourish and fall,
And the Gods of the Copybook Headings, I notice, outlast them all.
We were living in trees when they met us. They showed us each in turn

That Water would certainly wet us, as Fire would
certainly burn:
But we found them lacking in Uplift, Vision and
Breadth of Mind,
So we left them to teach the Gorillas while we
followed the March of Mankind.
We moved as the Spirit listed. They never altered
their pace,
Being neither cloud nor wind-borne like the Gods of
the Market Place,
But they always caught up with our progress, and
presently word would come
That a tribe had been wiped off its icefield, or the
lights had gone out in Rome.
With the Hopes that our World is built on they were
utterly out of touch,
They denied that the Moon was Stilton; they denied
she was even Dutch;
They denied that Wishes were Horses; they denied
that a Pig had Wings;
So we worshipped the Gods of the Market Who
promised these beautiful things.
When the Cambrian measures were forming, They
promised perpetual peace.
They swore, if we gave them our weapons, that the
wars of the tribes would cease.
But when we disarmed They sold us and delivered us
bound to our foe,
And the Gods of the Copybook Headings said: "Stick
to the Devil you know."
On the first Feminian Sandstones we were promised
the Fuller Life
(Which started by loving our neighbour and ended by
loving his wife)

*Till our women had no more children and the men
    lost reason and faith,*

*And the Gods of the Copybook Headings said: "The
    Wages of Sin is Death."*

*In the Carboniferous Epoch we were promised abun-
    dance for all,*

By robbing selected Peter to pay for collective Paul;

*But, though we had plenty of money, there was
    nothing our money could buy,*

*And the Gods of the Copybook Headings said: "If you
    don't work you die."*

*Then the Gods of the Market tumbled, and their
    smooth-tongued wizards withdrew*

*And the hearts of the meanest were humbled and
    began to believe it was true*

*That All is not Gold that Glitters, and Two and Two
    make Four*

*And the Gods of the Copybook Headings limped up to
    explain it once more.*

As it will be in the future, it was at the birth of Man

*There are only four things certain since Social
    Progress began.*

*That the Dog returns to his Vomit and the Sow
    returns to her Mire,*

*And the burnt Fool's bandaged finger goes wabbling
    back to the Fire;*

*And that after this is accomplished, and the brave
    new world begins*

*When all men are paid for existing and no man must
    pay for his sins,*

*As surely as Water will wet us, as surely as Fire will
    burn,*

*The Gods of the Copybook Headings with terror and
    slaughter return!*

"Father explained that to me once," Robert said.

"What does it mean, Robert?" Roger asked him.

"It's talking about how people keep doing stupid things in spite of what the wise sayings, the kind that show up at the top of your papers at school, keep telling you."

"Well, it's deep, anyway," Geoffrey said.

"You're not too bad a chap when you get enough lickings," Robert said.

Geoffrey flushed. "Your aunt!"

"Can't mouth off around her," Roger said.

"That's not the licking you were upset about, though," Robert said, and Geoffrey flushed.

"Just because Roger... Yes, I know, I was supposed to be watching him... anyway, just because I mismeasured that board..."

"Expensive board," Robert said. "One inch too short..."

"Is as good as a mile," Geoffrey finished the saying. "He kept that board on top of the scrap pile all day," Geoffrey said. "I felt it staring at me. Well, except when we were working inside, which we were doing mostly today. I must have climbed in and out of a window a hundred times today."

"Boards can't stare at you," Roger said.

"It's an expression, Dinkus!" Geoffrey said, and hurled a shoe at him.

"What was that?" Aunt Grace asked, coming in.

"I'm sorry, Mrs Livingston, that was me hurling a shoe at Roger."

"Well, he probably deserved it, but my walls don't!"

"Yes, ma'am," he said and watched, relieved, as she stomped out.

"I thought you were going to catch it for sure," Roger said.

"If he hadn't fessed up, he would have," Robert said.

"I think she's gotten soft since Mr Thacker started paying for her," Geoffrey said.

"That's a funny way to put it," Roger said.

"Well, how do you put it?" Geoffrey asked. "She set him a price, and he's paying it."

"As are we," Robert said. "We've been working, what, five weeks? Although I don't mind. I think it will be good for our business, her marrying him."

"Maybe she'll turn out another nipper or two," Geoffrey said.

"Nah, she's too old," Roger said.

"Don't let her catch you saying that," Geoffrey said.

"Saying what?" said Esther, coming in, followed by Ruth.

"Oh, nothing," Robert said. "What do you need?"

"Aunt says she's got some work to do, and you should say our prayers," Esther said.

"Very well, go back and I'll be in in a minute."

———

"Geoffrey?" Roger heard, and Geoffrey trotted over to where Mr Thacker was standing. He saw Mr Thacker hand him an envelope; Geoffrey try to refuse, and then accept the envelope even while shaking his head. Then he saw Mr Thacker kept talking to him.

"What do you suppose they are talking about?"

"Mr Thacker is telling him he did a good job on the house," Robert said. "And paying him. He told me about it."

"Will he pay us?"

"Don't be silly," Robert said, "You don't get paid for working on your own house."

"Guess not," Roger said, disappointed. "How much did he give him?"

"He didn't tell me, and, no, don't ask. That's between him and Mr Thacker."

Geoffrey came hurrying over. "He paid me!"

"Yeah, we knew that."

"I didn't! My father never said anything about my getting paid! He just said that it would be a good deed to help build a house for..." he trailed off, beet red.

"It's OK," Robert said, putting his arm around Geoffrey's shoulder. "We know we're orphans. He spent a long time talking to you."

"He got me another job!" Geoffrey said, shaking Robert's arm off and turning to face the other boys. "Said as how he ran into Mr Parker at the store, and he was talking about building a house for his son, who is gonna get hitched to Missy Grant, who I will be glad to see out of our class. So Mr Thacker said that I do good enough work for a boy, that I'd been working for him for six weeks and showed up every day. Not a hard worker," he said, blushing, "But as how I was careful, smart, and not too slow to learn things. He even said he mentioned that one board just to show I learned my lesson and... and took my licking like a man and didn't do it again. Said it was the only time he had to do it."

"Well, now, that's true," Robert said. "At least about learning your lesson."

Geoffrey shoved him, grinning, and Robert shoved him back, and then they both turned to look at the addition.

"You going home tonight?" Roger asked when it didn't look like the big boys would fight.

"Nah, Father didn't know we would get done so soon, so he sent my church stuff with me yesterday. I won't mind getting some of your Ma's dinner."

"She can cook," Roger said. "Almost as good as she can lick."

"We better go get washed off and change, then," Geoffrey said, "or she won't let us in to dinner."

The way to love anything is to realize that it may be lost.
— Gilbert K. Chesterton

Chapter Eleven

THE OLD GUY

It was a very quiet day, which Geoffrey liked. His life had been a bit too busy recently. He still wasn't sure how he felt about being friends with the Bobtails. Especially since it meant hanging around their Aunt Grace who was the only woman in the town who would lick him. He had to be careful around several of the men, but...

He heard the noise of the crackling of some bushes and looked to see some old guy pushing himself through them and over to his spot. Well, the other side of the same pond. Funny looking old guy, floppy hat with fishing flies stuck in it, casual shirt, loose denim pants, and some kind of canvas shoes. Tromping into Geoffrey's spot as if he owned it.

Geoffrey sighed and began picking up his stuff. He didn't want to share his spot with no old man, and, besides, it was the first really hot day after that long spring they had had, and he wanted to do some swimming pretty soon, and no fisherman worth his salt wanted some kid mucking about in...

"Sit down, young man; I have some questions for you," the old man said, with the kind of voice that made his backside tingle.

Geoffrey hadn't really stood up, but he sat back down and wiggled his pole around, hoping for a bite. He hated that this guy had caught him here in just an old pair of shorts; as a preacher's kid, he had a duty to dress proper, and there was nothing proper about these old shorts. They were the kind of thing any common kid might wear. Some of 'em might even wear better than this!

"I understand that you are the son of the local preacher?" the old man asked.

Geoffrey looked up. The old guy was arranging his things along the bank, including a rather large hamper. Looked like he had brought himself a good dinner, while Geoffrey had only thrown a sandwich into a paper bag.

"Yes, sir," Geoffrey answered, not really wanting to talk to this old geezer and not happy with the choice of subjects. Being a preacher's kid was a pain. If only his Pa were a regular fellow like the other boys. But then Geoffrey himself would just be a common kid, which he didn't want either.

"And you know the new children in town? Robert, Esther, Roger and Ruth?"

Geoffrey stared at the man. "The Bobtails? Can't say I know Ruth much; she doesn't come to school yet nor talk neither. And Esther's a girl. Know the boys well enough, I reckon." What kind of old man was this? Not asking about how the fish were biting or anything, but about local gossip. Stupid old man.

"And are you a friend of theirs?"

Geoffrey laughed, "Up until a while ago, I guess I was the person they hated most in the whole world, after the person who fixed the gas at their folk's house."

"But now?"

Geoffrey stared at the man. This was taking even gossip a bit far. But, respect for elders and all that. "We get along now. Mostly. Did some work together."

"That's good. And how are they doing?"

"Don't reckon that's none of your business," This was going way too far. Who was this geezer to come around asking questions about his friends or anyone in their town?

"Young man, it is very much my business, and I will ask you not to get brazen with me. Now, how are they doing?"

Geoffrey stared at him. How could it possibly be any business of his? But he didn't seem to be the type that would lie about such a thing, so, well, Geoffrey didn't always understand adults and their ways. "They're doing well enough, I reckon. As well as they could be, seeing as how their folks died, and they had to come live with Mrs Livingston."

"She doesn't treat them well?"

"Treat them well? What are you talking about, mister? She treats them fine. Not someone I'd want for my mother, but we can't all have the same mother... or aunt or whatever. She treats them fine. They get plenty to eat, go to school regular and have lessons at home too."

"She keeps them in order?"

"Mister, ain't nobody ever been kept in as good order as Mrs Livingston keeps them. They all get licked plenty regular, and mostly fair, too. Roger mostly. He's that type."

"The oldest boy, Robert, is getting older. Do you think she will be able to keep him in order when he grows?"

"He is getting taller," Geoffrey admitted. "But she'll keep him in fine order if he grows to be a seven-foot man grown. And besides, she's about to get hitched to Mr Thacker, so even if she couldn't, he could. He raised kids himself, older than me, grown and gone and all, but he raised them fine."

"When are they getting married?"

"When he finishes the addition to her house, which he

pretty much is. So I figure he'll be moving in any day now. Dunno if they've talked to my dad; he doesn't tell me that kind of thing. Although, they've both been married before, so maybe they don't want a bunch of fuss. Neither one seems the type."

"Do you think they will do well, married?"

"I reckon. He pinches her bottom all the time, which takes a bit of gumption, man doing that to Mrs Livingston. Reckon they'll do well enough, maybe have a couple more kids."

Before the old man could respond to this revelation, his line bobbed down and, quick as a wink, that old man jerked his rod and, a couple of minutes later, had a nice big fish all landed on the bank.

The old man looked at it. "I'm afraid I am not going to have time to cook this," he said. "Would you like it? In payment for my questions?"

"Would I!" Geoffrey said, and hurried over, slid his keeper rope through the fish's gills and tossed it back in the water. "That was a good fish, mister," he said, once it was safely on his, Geoffrey's, line.

"It was indeed," the old man said, getting up and arranging his things. "But I consider our exchange more than fair."

Geoffrey watched the old man walk away and then went back to his place, trailing his keeper string behind him. That had been strange. Man comes and gets all ready to fish and eat and all and then up and leaves. But now that Geoffrey had three fish on his line, it was time for a swim.

Robert hauled on the reins, and the buggy stopped almost right in front of the store. He jumped down and went to the back of the buggy, checked the tag carefully, picked up the cheese, and walked in the store.

"Cheese delivery, Mr Johnson," he called out.

"Oh, Robert, good, you are here. This gentleman was looking for you, and I told him you would be in soon."

Robert plunked the cheese on the counter and turned to the man. An older man, wearing pretty old, casual clothes. Possibly a tourist. "You want some cheese, Sir? We have several kinds; cottage cheese, soft spreadable local, aged cheddar..."

"Yes, possibly. You make them yourself?"

"I do milking and deliveries, mostly. Sometimes I churn. Mostly my aunt and my sister do the work on the cheese. They keep the whole thing clean, if you're worried about that, Sir."

"I'm sure they do. You say you have soft spreadable... well, no, I'm travelling, perhaps cheddar would be better."

"Travels well, cheddar," Robert agreed. "I have some in the buggy in a cooler; people often stop me on the way."

"I think I will," the old man said. "You say your aunt makes it? You live with her?"

Robert's face flushed just a bit. "Yes, sir, she took us in when our folks died."

"That was good of her."

"Yes, sir, powerful good."

"Well, let us look at this cheese," the old man said.

After the man had bought his cheese and Robert went back in the store, Mr Johnson looked at him curiously. "Did you know him?"

"Never seen him before in my life," Robert said, counting the money Mr Johnson had left for him on the counter.

"It was strange. He seemed to know you. Asked if I knew you and your siblings. Asked how you were doing."

"Must have heard about the cheese," Robert said. "We get

tourists stop by the house from time to time. Geoffrey sold some the other day," he said, grinning. "Was most put out, but he was the only one of us that had clean hands, so we sent him to greet the buggy. Did a good job, though, sold quite a bit."

"Well, I suppose," Mr Johnson said doubtfully. "But he didn't talk about the cheese until I mentioned it."

"Well, he bought cheese," Robert said, pocketing the money and heading for the door. He had more deliveries to make, and he didn't want to be late getting home, and he didn't much care about old men buying cheese as long as he sold it right. His aunt wouldn't lick him for being late from deliveries, she knew how some people would talk, but he still liked to be on time.

"I'll see you next week, Robert," Mr Johnson said. "And bring a new crock of the soft spreadable; I'm running low."

Robert stopped and made a note in his order book. "Next week," he agreed, and went out.

Jonathon Thacker watched the stern-looking older man ride up, wondering what on earth he was doing here. He didn't look like anyone who would be buying hay or needing a horse bred.

"Good afternoon," the old man said, getting down from his horse as if he expected to stay a spell. "I have some questions to ask you."

"I'm kind of busy," Jonathon said, not really wanting to play the tourist guide. The man's accent was not from around here, certainly.

"You will have time to answer these questions, I assure you," the old man said, with the kind of voice that just expected you to listen to him.

"If you say so," Jonathon said. "Let's go in and have ourselves something to eat, anyway, so as to not waste time."

Jonathon went in and poured them both coffee and got out some of those doughnuts that Esther had cooked. They were fine doughnuts, if not all of them were exactly even.

"Well, go ahead with your questions," Jonathon said, seating himself down.

"I am here about the Bobtails," the old man said, and Jonathon sat up.

"I don't see how they are any of your business."

"The people in this area seem to be all of one mind on that," the old man replied with a bit of a grin. "I paid a fish one time I asked these questions. But as I told the young man down at the fishing hole, I can assure you that these questions are very much my business."

"Now," he said, "I understand you are to marry Mrs Livingston?"

"We are firm betrothed," Jonathon said. "She set me a task, and I finished it."

"I see. And did you court her long?"

"Well, when my wife died two years ago, I told Mrs Livingston as how we should get married. She told me she had no need of a husband. But when she took in those young'ens, well, I told her she did now. So when she made protest her house wasn't big enough... and we will need to live in her house, as moving her dairy things would be powerful difficult... why I said if that was her only objection, I would build an addition. I don't think she expected me to take her quite so literal, but she gave in quick enough."

"She has a dairy, and I have hay fields, and I breed horses, so together we will be doing very well."

"I see. And how is she doing with the children?"

"She's doing just fine, but children need a father."

"Quite. But you have no complaint of how they are being treated now?"

"Certainly not. She gives them more food than they ate back in town, work to go with it, keeps them firm in line."

"And they are being adequately disciplined? Do they get enough sleep?"

"Discipline? You must not know Grace at all. And they fall asleep exhausted every evening, I'm sure. Never see bags under their eyes."

"And their spiritual care?"

"They never miss a Sunday at church unless they're sick, and she has her oldest, Robert, doing their devotions every day. That's one thing she needs me for, and I do it sometimes when I'm there. But Robert is learning it well."

"Excellent. I have some documents you and your new wife will need to sign. I already have the rest of the signatures I need."

Bober

This triangle of truisms, of father, mother and child, cannot be destroyed; it can only destroy those civilisations which disregard it.
— **Gilbert K. Chesterton**

Chapter Twelve

THE KITCHEN

Mrs Grace Livingston heard the sound of the wagon in the yard and sighed. She had work to do! He couldn't always be coming over.

Well, that wasn't really fair. He had mostly come over to work on the addition, bring furniture and the like. He wouldn't leave without interrupting her, it was true, but she supposed that, too, was fair in a man about to get a new wife. Certainly, it was what...

The kitchen door banged open, and she turned, startled. It wasn't at all like him to just come barging in. And... and the look on his face. And what was he holding up? Some paper?

Dazed at this bizarre behaviour, she went over and he thrust it at her. She started reading...

Know all men present that this represents the final judgement of this court concerning the adoption and residue estate declaration for the estate of ...

Her eyes skimmed frantically down the page...

... are hereby finally and completely released into the custody of Grace Thacker, aka Livingston nee Barker and her husband, Jonathon Thacker...

She shrieked. There could be no other word for it, and almost as soon as it was out of her mouth, she clamped down. What would the children think? What would Jonathon think?

But before she even had a chance to look at him, the other door opened and all four children came tumbling in, Roger, as usual, in the lead.

"Aunt Grace?" Esther said, no doubt shocked at her extremely untoward behaviour. Why, she was crying! "Aunt Grace, what is it?"

Before she even had a chance to determine what was best to say, let alone have a chance to compose herself enough to say it, Jonathon took the paper from her and thrust it out at Robert.

Robert read it out loud to everyone, slowly and carefully, but Grace had very little chance to listen as Jonathon was behaving most inappropriately, having come behind her and with his hands... most inappropriately. But she couldn't find the words to rebuke him; she was too busy crying and most inappropriately behaving herself.

Robert finished and looked at her curiously. "I never knew there was any question."

"Question of what?" Roger said, grabbing an apple from the table and biting into it.

Esther came and hugged her, crying herself, while Ruth merely watched, confused. But Grace was glad to see her hand *not* go into her mouth.

"I... I sent him a letter, every week," Grace said. "But I never knew he was... when he was..." she sputtered off, horribly embarrassed at how out of control she was acting.

"We will put this on our kitchen wall," Jonathon declared, taking the paper back from Robert and, spying a spare nail, pushed it up. "So we can always see it."

"And," he added, coming back behind her and moving his

hands even more inappropriately, "I will take you all out to dinner in the big town tonight. Go and put your best clothes on."

The children all hurriedly left, and Grace finally found the words to object to his behaviour. "Jonathon! We are not yet husband and wife. You need to control yourself..."

"Ah, but we are," he said, hugging her even tighter. "I don't need to control myself, and I'm not going to control myself. Didn't you read the document, signed by a judge and everything? I am now your husband and the father of those children just as you are now their mother, and you better not forget either one."

"As if I would!" Grace said.

The End

NOTES

PROLOGUE

1. Nieces and Nephews

2. THE HOUSE

1. https://archive.org/details/savourypastrysa00vinegoog/page/n18/mode/2up
2. https://www.gutenberg.org/files/32393/32393-h/32393-h.htm
3. By Pike and Dike by GA Henty

6. THE SCHOOLROOM

1. https://www.gutenberg.org/files/236/236-h/236-h.htm
2. https://www.gutenberg.org/files/1661/1661-h/1661-h.htm#chap03

7. WORK

1. The Science of Cooking, page 28

8. THE STORM

1. Father goose poetry by Baum: https://babel.hathitrust.org/cgi/pt?id=hvd.32044011617800&view=1up&seq=18
2. Charles Haddon Spurgeon January 1, 1970
     Scripture: Hosea 14:3
     From: Metropolitan Tabernacle Pulpit Volume 28

ACKNOWLEDGMENTS

Additional Artist Contributions

Thank you to all my young illustrators, who did such an amazing job!

- Arthur

ABOUT THE AUTHOR

Arthur Yeomans likes to write, and loves to read. He likes to write for his family, write about family, and read to his family. He likes to write about family, marriage, having children, raising children... and how God can and should be glorified in all of those things. He has a large family, has had several jobs and has lived in several countries, all of which bring their own influence to his writing.

Follow the author on his website:
www.ArthurYeomans.com

BOBTAILS ADVENTURES SERIES

Also in the three-volume series by Arthur Yeomans:

The Bobtails and the Cousins

Now that the adoption is final, and the addition complete, the
Bobtails invite their cousins to come for a visit to their new home.
Of course, life on a dairy farm with Aunt Grace and Mr Thacker is
not exactly everyone's cup of tea.

Coming Summer 2023

———————

The Bobtails Go to France

Aunt Grace learned all of her cheese recipes from her mother-in-law.
When her dead husband's aunt dies, she has to go to to France to
pick up her inheritance: the families secret cheese recipe and
culture. But Mr Thacker decides they should all go.

Coming Christmas 2023